I0549100

Managansett Press

Don D'Ammassa is the author of:

Horror
Blood Beast
Servant of Chaos*
Caverns of Chaos*
Wings over Manhattan
The Gargoyle
That Way Madness Lies*
Little Evils*
Passing Death*
Date with the Dark*
The Devil Is in the Details*
Living Things*
Shadows Over R'Lyeh*

Science Fiction
Scarab*
Haven*
Narcissus*
Translation Station
The Sinking Island*
Alien & Otherwise*
Wormdance*
Sandcastles*
Carbon Copies*

Mysteries
Murder in Silverplate*
Dead of Winter*
Death at the Art Gallery*
Death on the Mountain*
Death on Black Island*
Death in Black and Whtie*

Fantasy
The Kaleidoscope*
Elaborate Lies*
The Maltese Gargoyle*
Perilous Pursuits*
Multiplicity*

Nonfiction
The Encyclopedia of Science Fiction
The Encyclopedia of Fantasy and Horror
The Encyclopedia of Adventure Fiction
Masters of Detection Vol I*
Masters of Detection Vol II*
Masters of Detection Vol III*
Architects of Tomorrow Vol I*

*published by Managansett Press

PHANTOM OF THE SPACE OPERA

"Corruption in Office" first appeared in *The Ultimate Zombie*, 1993

"The Daylight Vampire" first appeared in *Haunts*, 1993

"Dumb Genius" first appeared in *Terra Incognita*, 2000

"Hair Apparent" first appeared in *100 Wicked Witch Stories*, 1995

"Homework" first appeared in *Analog*, 1992

"The Last Demon" first appeared in *Blood Lite 3*, 2012

"Milk Curdling Horror" first appeared in *Deathrealm*, 1996

"No Problem: first appeared in *Blood Lite*, 2008

"The Phantom of the Space Opera" first appeared in *The Ultimate Alien* (1995)

"Stakeout" first appeared in *Horrors: 365 Scary Stories*, 1998

"The Subterrine, or 20,000 Leagues Under the Soil" first appeared in *Space & Time*, 1993

"Thoracic Park" first appeared in *Analog*, 1996

All other stories appear for the first time and are copyright 2015.

Managansett Press First Edition 2015

PHANTOM OF THE SPACE OPERA

CONTENTS

THE PHANTOM OF THE SPACE OPERA

A chorus line of mini-skirted mice danced their way across the room as Polonius collapsed in a pool of blood.

"Goddamn it! The director waved his arms disgustedly, although he was secretly pleased that the holographic projector had chosen that precise moment to malfunction. He turned to the new captain of the *Gaston Leroux*. "That's what we've had to deal with ever since we opened on Harmony, eight stops back, either during rehearsals like this or in the middle of an actual performance. The image addressing system has broken down and we keep getting bits and pieces from other productions. Those are from one of the children's programs," he explained unnecessarily, gesturing toward the mice, who blinked out of existence as though they'd been cued.

Jak Debienne sighed. "I can understand your frustration, Fulton. Captain Philippe included some of the unfortunate details in his resignation, Lady Godiva making an appearance in *Faust*, for example. And leprechauns in *Gone with the Wind*."

"Little green Martians."

"I beg your pardon?"

"It was little green Martians in *Gone with the Wind*. The leprechauns were in Pygmalion. And we had a pair of dinosaurs pop up during the chariot race from *Ben Hur*."

"In any case, I've brought an expert with me. Mr. Shagny comes highly recommended. I'm sure he'll have no difficulty correcting the situation once we're aboard the *Leroux*."

"Can't be soon enough for me. Medea has the most unforgiving audiences on our entire tour, and they weren't amused when Banquo's ghost showed up in *A Streetcar Named Desire* yesterday."

"Understandably." But Debienne's thoughts were already elsewhere, metaphorically in space, where his new command maintained a geosynchronous orbit above the theater. He had mixed

7

feelings about this assignment. On the one hand, the *Leroux* was a proud ship with three centuries of history; on the other, it was old, its equipment obsolete and untrustworthy, built on a scale and to a design that no one had ever replicated. And there were disturbing stories.

"Fulton, did you know Captain Philippe very well?"

"The Captain? Oh, as well as any, I suppose. He was never one to do much socializing. A good man, though. We were all sorry to see him go." Fulton suddenly flushed. "Not that we aren't looking forward to working with you, of course."

Debienne ignored the faux pas. "But he was under a great deal of stress lately, wasn't he?"

"No more than usual. I mean, we've been having problems since before he came aboard. When it isn't the holo equipment, it's the air spargers, or communications, or something else. The <u>Leroux</u> is a beautiful ship, sir, but aging, the parts wearing out."

"Yes, I understand that, but Captain Philippe told me...well, to be perfectly honest, he told me the <u>Leroux</u> was haunted."

Fulton's eyebrows rose. "Oh, he told you about the ghost. Some of us were wondering whether he'd warn you or leave it up to the rest of us."

The captain blinked. "But surely you don't believe such nonsense. You're an intelligent man."

Fulton nodded. "And smart enough to accept the truth. There's an unseen presence aboard the <u>Leroux</u>, Captain, and it's been there for three hundred years. I don't know if it's a ghost, but it's real."

Clearly Debienne found the concept unacceptable. "And Captain Philippe actually kept a monitor set aside for the use of this...presence? And allowed it access to the main computers?"

"That he did. And so did Captains Marques and Sandoval and Nkruma and Fukora before him, and all the others too, I imagine."

"Well this is one tradition that ends now."

Mercifully, the final performance on Medea went without incident. As soon as the audience had filed out, technicians killed the holographic projectors and the replica of Carnegie Hall vanished, revealing the oversized collapsible dome that had actually sheltered the production. An hour later, even the dome was gone, loaded about the cargo shuttle, lifted into orbit after the quartermaster reconciled his inventory.

As soon as he was aboard, Debienne used his access code to formally assume command of the Leroux, addressed the entire crew briefly, then met with the senior staff.

"I know that you've had to deal with inadequate equipment lately, and I won't pretend we can afford to replace it all. But I do have some good news. Mr. Shagny here," and a tall, dark haired young man rose and nodded around the room, "is going to overhaul our computers while we're enroute to Callypygia. That should at least clear up the problems with the holos and probably some of the other glitches as well. Unfortunately, that means rewriting portions of the main memory, including the security system. You'll all be assigned new passwords when Mr. Shagny is finished."

There was an uneasy stirring around the room. Debienne frowned. "Is there a problem? Speak up, please."

"Sir," the executive officer shifted her weight nervously from one foot to the other, "it's just, well, we were wondering what you were planning to do about the ghost, sir." She glanced across the room to where Fulton stood with crossed arms, chewing his moustache.

"I respect shipboard traditions as much as anyone, so long as they don't interfere with the smooth operation of this command. That doesn't include allocating valuable computer time to a fanciful spirit, if that's what you're asking."

"But, sir..."

He raised his hand, halting her in mid-word. "This is not a debatable issue, Major Poligny. If our ghostly passenger has a problem, he can take it up with me personally. Now if you'll all excuse me, it's been a long day."

But Captain Debienne found it more difficult to rest than he'd anticipated. Someone had entered his private quarters, even though the door had been reset to respond only to his own distinctive DNA signature.

His spare uniforms had all been dyed fluorescent orange.

"That should do it." Rollo Shagny sat back from the console, watched confidently as the monitor displayed a stream of confirmation messages. "There might still be a few small problems with the subsidiary systems, but the main logic boards are all re-integrated."

Captain Debienne nodded, but without enthusiasm. Shagny's rapid success debugging the malfunctioning computers was one of the few positive elements of the past several ship days. No matter what he ordered from the replicator, it always delivered something different, the artificial gravity in his quarters cut off at unpredictable intervals, and he'd twice been sprayed with fire retardant foam for no discernible reason. No one else aboard was experiencing such difficulties, and Shagny's diagnostics had yet to identify the problem.

"Excellent work, Mr. Shagny. And with two days to spare." The technician was scheduled to leave the *Leroux* at its next port of call.

"I was meaning to talk to you about that, Captain." Shagny seemed unsure of himself, his voice faltering. "I'd like to stay on for a while, at least until the peripherals have been checked out. I could book passage back from New Paris or Chaney."

Debienne sighed. "I don't suppose it would do any good to tell you you're wasting your time."

"Sir?"

"Miss Dai is quite determined to remain aboard the *Leroux*, Shagny, despite what I'm told is an unremarkable singing voice."

"It's just that she's never had a chance..." The younger man stopped in mid-sentence, realized he was fooling no one.

Debienne gestured dismissively. "Yes, yes, I'm sure you're right. But so long as Scarlotta is aboard, Dai will have to make do with secondary parts. I know the woman's personality leaves something to be desired, but she has a magnificent voice. In any case, we'll be happy to enjoy your company for as long as you choose to remain with us, Mr. Shagny."

"Thank you, sir."

"Sorry, rehearsals are closed today." The burly crewman didn't sound as though he was sorry. Shagny turned away without answering and made his way back to the main corridor.

Rollo Shagny had always found it easier to interact with computers than with people. They were so much more predictable. Although convinced that Kristin Dai was the woman destined to be his wife, he recognized that so far she was barely aware of his existence. And now he couldn't even watch her from a distance.

Frustrated, he kicked out at a pile of old ropes someone had dumped in the passageway.

"Hey! What'd I ever do to you?"

Shagny stepped back as the ropes uncoiled revealing a gnarled central trunk. "My God, you're a Persean!"

"Is that any reason to assault me?"

"No, of course not. I'm deeply sorry. I didn't know..."

The ropelike tentacles flexed several times, then slowly recoiled around the creature's core. "No harm done. You're the programming genius, aren't you?"

"I don't know about the genius part, but I'm Rollo Shagny."

"Pleased to meet you, friend Shagny. My name is..." What followed was a string of clicks and whistles totally beyond the capabilities of human vocal chords. "But to my human friends, I'm just the Persean."

"You're a member of the troupe then?" There were a handful of alien performers aboard, although the _Leroux_ rarely visited non-human worlds.

"Hardly. No, I'm rather a special case. I was one of the investors who financed the _Leroux_ when it was being assembled in orbit above Gwydion. I never sold my share when the company bought controlling interest."

"You were alive when the ship was built?" Shagny remained skeptical. "That was almost three hundred years ago."

"Three hundred and five, actually, and I was past my youth even then. But I owed a favor to Erak, the ship's designer, and he was short on credit at a critical stage in the project. Turned out to be a pretty good investment, gave me a place to put down roots, so to speak." Shagny glanced toward the deck, noticed his companion did seem to stand on a cluster of spatulate roots.
    "

Their visit to Callypygia was a disaster from the outset. Fulton had chosen to open with an operetta, the inimitable Scarlotta singing the role of Madame Mimeo in _Rivets Revisited_. Debienne was monitoring the landing of the first cargo shuttle when Scarlotta herself stormed onto the bridge.

"Captain Debienne, I demand that you do something about this...this indignity!"

"Now what?" As far as Captain Debienne was concerned, all the indignities since he'd come aboard had been his and his alone. Even Shagny had been unable to suggest how those strange messages kept appearing in his personal data queue, a succession of vague threats and exhortations to honor the commitments of his predecessors.

"I found this on my terminal this morning." She held out a hard copy of a very brief message.

"You would be well advised," it read, "to develop a headache before today's performance. The role does not suit you." It was signed "The Ghost".

Two hours later, a defiant but clearly nervous Scarlotta was aboard the shuttle that carried the performers down to the surface. Debienne remained on the bridge, nervously aware that this would be the first test of Shagny's work on the holographic system.

"What's the problem there?" One of the monitoring stations was unoccupied although two of the technicians were sitting side by side at another.

"It's a spare, sir," explained Major Poligny, her voice faltering. "We only use it as a backup."

Debienne glanced around the bridge. "Very transparent, ladies and gentlemen. It's the ghost's monitor, isn't that right? Now stop this nonsense and man that station."

There was uncertain movement, as each crewmember waited for someone else to take up the position.

"All right, you spineless squidges," Debienne roared. "You! DeSouza! Come up here and take over my monitor. I'll risk the ghost's wrath if the rest of you haven't the stomach for it." Having mixed his biological metaphors adequately, Debienne moved to the unattended monitor.

He was standing there when Scarlotta started her first major solo.

Truly her voice was a magnificent instrument, her throat and vocal chords surgically altered to achieve the best possible compromise between range and tone. Her stage presence held the bridge crew's attention, particularly once the transformation started.

It was all a hologrammatic projection, of course, but the metamorphosis from a human being to a Tregonnian pufferfrog was quite cleverly animated. The superimposed image was not visible to Scarlotta herself, but the audience and the other performers could see it quite clearly. To give them credit, they didn't actually begin to laugh until the creature starting using a prehensile tongue to pick vermin out its fur.

That was just about the same time Captain Debienne was knocked unconscious by a power surge mysteriously diverted into his monitor.

Kristin Dai replaced Scarlotta for the next two performances, and surprised everyone by displaying a voice perhaps not as seasoned as it might be, but with a raw exuberance that clearly captured the attention of the audience. She explained afterward that she'd been using a new program, called The Muse, which she'd accidentally accessed while studying kibuki. Captain Debienne returned to the bridge in time to watch the final show, went directly to the command monitor, and never again mentioned the active but abandoned position.

That evening, he quietly asked Shagny to reinstate the ghost's password. Shagny wisely offered no comment.

For six days they orbited Callypygia, presenting a series of plays, ballets, operas, and concerts. Everything in their repertory was available on holodisk, and with better known performers, but the appeal of live performance art could not be denied. No matter where it travelled, the Leroux always played to a full house.

They were halfway to Eurydice when Kristin Dai disappeared.

"What do you mean they can't find her?" Shagny paced back and forth, unable to remain still.

Debienne sympathized with the younger man's frustration, shared it to a degree. "You have to remember, the Leroux is the size of a small city. There are miles and miles of corridors just in the inhabited sections, and there's fully a third of the ship that's maintained by remotes and without human intervention. Even the schematics in the master files aren't always accurate; there have been modifications over the years that went unrecorded. Hopefully, she has simply wandered off and gotten lost, and sooner or later she'll stumble across a working comset or a familiar landmark."

Unconvinced, Rollo Shagny joined a search party, tormented by visions of the lovely Kristin wandering alone in some abandoned stretch of corridor.

Kristin Dai was not alone.

She woke in unfamiliar surroundings, a small compartment apparently designed for temporary storage. The sleeping unit upon which she'd been lying was clean and comfortable, but primitive, lacking mood inducers. She sat up, examining her surroundings while she tried to remember how she'd come to be here.

The room was cluttered and dusty. Storage capsules were stacked in one corner, most of them empty. An enormous pile of rubbish dominated the opposite end of the room, completely covered by a litter of old theatrical masks, blocking what appeared to be the only exit.

Kristin stood up, paused while her head stopped spinning, then started toward the door.

"I'm afraid I can't allow you to leave just yet."

The voice was startling, deep and solemn, not unfriendly but terrifying for the simple reason that she could not identify its source. She appeared to be alone in the room, which offered no place of concealment.

"Who are you? Why have you brought me here?"

There was a sound which she thought might possibly be a sigh. "My name is Erak, although you know me as The Muse."

"The Muse? But that's..."

"A computer program? That's what I'd hoped you would believe." The voice originated somewhere near the door, a hidden speaker perhaps.

"But then, who are you?"

"I'm your mentor, Kristin, your friend, your admirer. Perhaps, once you come to understand me, your lover."

Despite the ambiguity of her situation, Kristin was intrigued. She took another tentative step forward. "Why are you hiding from me? Why talk from a distance?"

"Oh, but I'm right here, Kristin. Didn't you know?" And the pile of presumed rubbish stirred and moved in her direction.

Kristin gasped and shrank back, realizing the truth as the mound of refuse emerged from the shadows. Except that it was not a pile of discarded trash at all, but a living creature about twice her mass, its shape indeterminate because of the mesh of plaster masks that completely covered the clearly alien body.

Kristin Dai fainted for the first time in her life.

"I have been looking for you, my friend. We need to speak."

Shagny glanced to one side, saw the Persean emerging from a side corridor. The young man was exhausted and disheveled, having spent most of the last shipday searching fruitlessly through unfamiliar parts of the *Leroux.*

*"I'm really rather busy. Someon*e has gotten lost, you see, and..."

"The young lady, yes. But she is not lost."

Shagny hesitated. "What do you mean? Do you know where she is?"

"In a manner of speaking. She is with Erak."

"Erak?" The name sounded familiar but he couldn't quite place it. "I don't understand."

"That is because I have not yet explained. You see, a long time ago, before this ship had even been conceived of, I had a friend named Erak."

Shagny was in no mood for a long story and said so.

"Patience, my friend. Dai is in no immediate danger and it is important that you understand this if you are to help her."

Grudgingly, Shagny nodded acquiescence.

"Erak was in many ways unique. He was the runt of a litter sired by an individual he remembers only as the Brood Mother, a deformed mutation so bizarre that she sold him to a passing human starship collecting specimens for the interplanetary zoo on Caliban. There he was on exhibit for nearly a human century before he was able to convince his keepers that he was sentient. By then, information about his origin had been lost, and he was forced to resign himself to an existence completely separated from his own kind. Although, if his deformities were as massive as his memory indicates, that might have been just as well."

"What has all of this got to do with Kristin?" Shagny shifted his weight impatiently, anxious to resume his search.

The Persean ignored the interruption. "Once free, Erak set about integrating himself into a society dominated by your kind. Although several non-humans like myself have found a niche to occupy, Erak's physical form was so repulsive that he was finally forced to live in seclusion. Fortunately, his long lived nature allowed him to assimilate a broad range of engineering skills, culminating in the construction of the *Gaston Leroux*, the last project he completed before the anti-alien riots three centuries ago forced him into exile."

That's why Shagny remembered the name; the Persean had mentioned it when they first met.

"A very tragic story, but what has your long dead friend got to do with Kristin Dai?"

"Oh, Erak's not dead. He's still aboard the *Leroux*. I thought you'd realized that by now. And I believe he has abducted Kristin Dai."

"What...who are you?" Kristin had recovered to find herself once more lying on the small bed. Briefly she wondered how she'd gotten there, but her mind scampered away from too close consideration of that issue.

"My name is Erak, as I've just told you. And I am your greatest admirer. You have no reason to fear me."

She wasn't so sure of that, but the creature seemed to pose no immediate threat. Once again, she sat up, noticing that the ambulatory pile of masks was closer now, almost within reach.

"Would you like some music? I understand that humans frequently find it relaxing. I am actually quite good on the virtual organ."

"Why are you all covered up like that? Why won't you let me see what you look like?"

This time the sigh was unmistakable. "Because you would shrink from my horrid visage, Kristin. My face is the epitome of all ugliness, the ultimate shape of nausea, the essence of horribleness."

Kristin frowned. "Aren't you exaggerating a little?"

"Well, a little maybe. But it's pretty awful looking. Not that the rest of me is all that great either. The masks chafe at times, but they're light enough to be no more than a minor burden."

Touched despite lingering concern for her own safety, Kristin leaned forward. "It can't be that bad. I've travelled a lot, you know. We even performed on Nettlequass and Vroom, and we've had Squashages and Fumiteers in our company. I don't think I'd find your face all that revolting."

"Trust me, Kristin. It's better if you don't."

But curiosity had gotten the best of her and Kristin reached out suddenly, grasped the mask from behind which Erak's voice seemed to originate, and ripped it free.

It was pretty bad, but she was a trained actress, maintained her composure, spoke through gritted teeth. "See, I told you your face wouldn't upset me that much."

"That's not my face. That's an elbow."

Her expression crumpled a bit. "Oh. Well, then..." And before doubts could build, she reached out again, pulled off a large smiley face. It was worse, but not much worse than the elbow. This time she was forced to look away, but only long enough to realize how thoughtless she was being. "I've seen worse," she lied.

"That's not my face either."

"It's not? But the nose..."

"That's not a nose. That's...well, let's just say it's not something I'd reveal even among my own kind. Care to try again?"

"No, I think you've made your point."

"Are you sure this is the way?" Shagny was having second thoughts about this expedition. The Persean had already led him through a circuitous route deep into the automated regions of the Leroux.

"There are more direct routes, but Erak will have taken precautions against direct assaults. He's a very private being, friend Rollo, and has certainly set safeguards to repel intruders."

"How could he have been here all this time without ever doing anything that would make someone suspect that he was aboard?"

"He couldn't have. He needs access to the computer to divert supplies, and to ensure that his lair remains hidden. Erak has been quite active. Surely you've realized by now that he's the ghost."

It made sense. "All right, I can accept that. But why Kristin? They're not even the same species."

"No, but I imagine that after several centuries of chastity, he must be feeling considerable frustration. And after all, Erak was raised in a human society, and he necessarily absorbed human concepts of beauty."

The image that forced itself into Shagny's mind was a disturbing one.

They pressed on.

17

"They dare!"

The sound of anger transformed Erak from a tragic though undeniably repulsive figure into a creature of absolute menace.

"What is it?" Kristin drew back in alarm.

"The traitorous Persean has violated my trust. It has shown someone the way into my most secret chambers. It shall pay for its perfidy and he for his presumption." The door dilated open and Erak slithered through with a speed that quite surprised Kristin. But she was quick to follow, taking advantage of the chance for escape.

Outside, she blinked in confusion, finding herself in an unfamiliar environment filled with piping and cables and accesstubes. Erak was nowhere in sight but she heard his voice raging somewhere to her left, and cautiously followed, recognizing it as her only landmark in this mechanical maze.

When she finally located him, he was perched on a catwalk above a metallic chamber. Below, two figures moved restlessly from side to side, one apparently an ambulatory tree, the other the awkward young man she'd seen hanging around the rehearsal room.

"You've broken your last confidence my deciduous friend," Erak shouted, still not noticing that Kristin had joined them. "In a few moments, the backwash from the main drive will incinerate you down to your last seedpod, and this foolish young man as well."

"Where is Kristin?" Shagny shouted angrily from the chamber in which he'd been imprisoned. "Don't you dare to touch her, you fiend."

Kristin instantly realized the truth of the situation and hastened to Erak's side. "No! If you love me as you say you do, you'll spare them. They're only here because of me."

"They have trespassed on my domain. They lives are forfeit." But Erak's voice was already less certain.

Kristin pressed her advantage. "Release them. Allow me to see them safely back to the passenger quarters and I will return to you of my own free will. You have my promise."

For a moment it seemed that Erak would refuse, but instead his shoulders slumped - all six of them - and a tentacle reached out to a control panel. The chamber door irised.

"Take them then. But remember your promise to me."

"You can't go back, Kristin. I forbid it!" Shagny was beside himself with frustrated anger. "He's inhuman."

"That's true, but that's why I must go back. Don't you understand how lonely it must be for him, never to see another of his own kind, never even to know their nature?"

They'd argued the point several times already, but Kristin refused to budge. On the brink of despair, Shagny suddenly had an inspiration.

"All right then, but promise me this. You won't return to him until after we've left orbit around Eurydice."

Kristin frowned. "But I won't change my mind..."

"Perhaps not. Just promise me this short delay. I have something in mind."

Kristin surrendered. "All right. I don't suppose he'll mind waiting a few more days after all those centuries."

And so it was.

"Rollo, I've just come to say goodbye." She'd become quite fond of Shagny since his abortive attempt to rescue her. He could be quite charming really, when he was relaxed. If only she didn't feel morally obligated to Erak, Kristin thought their relationship might well take a more serious turn.

"I'm going with you."

"What?"

"You heard me. I'm going with you to see Erak. I have some information that might interest him."

It wasn't hard to find their way back. Erak sent out a modified maintenance robot to act as guide.

"Why do you intrude on our happiness?" The alien was clearly not happy to see Shagny again.

"Because I have something important to tell you. I've discovered the truth about your species."

Erak shook its head, or something anyway. "My species is unknown to your kind. Believe me, I have examined all the records."

"You checked all the records as of three centuries ago. We've expanded quite a lot since then. I uploaded the relevant information from Eurydice. Your home world is called Ichoria, and while your exact lineage remains a mystery, it is probable that you were born in the northern hemisphere."

There was a prolonged silence. "If that's true, I appreciate your telling me, but it has no effect on my situation. You forget, I am an outcast even from my own kind, a hideously deformed monster."

Shagny nodded. "I realize that and believe me, you have my sympathy. To a lesser degree, I know what it's like to be ostracized. But there's more."

"More?" Erak tapped something against the deckplates. Fingers?

"There was considerable information about the physiology of your species. I almost passed it by but something, fate perhaps, caused me to look into that as well. And I made a rather startling discovery." He paused dramatically.

"It would be best if you left the theatrics to those professionally trained," Erak said quietly. "What do you have to tell me."

"Simply this," Shagny intoned portentously. "Male Ichorians invariably die within their first century. They are genetically designed that way, to allow greater diversity in the gene pool. And since you've lived at least five times that long..."

There was a sudden, pregnant silence, broken finally when Erak completed the sentence. "...then I am female."

"Got it in one."

Rollo Shagny entered the turbolift, satisfied that his wooing of Kristin Dai was proceeding relatively successfully. She still hadn't agreed to leave the ship and settle down with him, but her resolve was weakening. By the time they reached Tannenbaum, he hoped to have won her over.

He was mentally preliving their wedding when he realized that the lift had dropped well below the level he'd asked for. Before he could react, a familiar voice issued from the speaker grill. Familiar, but subtly changed, softer.

"I hope you don't mind my forwardness, Rollo?"

"Erak? Is that you? What's going on?"

"Don't be disturbed, Rollo. You're not in any danger. Far from it. I just had to see you again. I know that you're hoping to convince Kristin to leave the *Leroux* with you, and I really think you should reconsider."

Shagny shook his head with disgust. "Listen, Erak, I thought we'd settled all this. Look, I'm sorry about your situation but it's not my fault and there's really nothing we can do about it. You must realize that Kristin has a life of her own to lead, and her future and yours are bound to be different."

"Yes, yes, I understand all that. It was a mistake and I regret the inconvenience I've caused her." There was a short pause, then a sound that might almost have been a sigh. "I was just wondering if you'd ever considered a change in profession. A life on the stage might help you to overcome your shyness. You're actually quite handsome, you know."

The turbolift plunged into the depths of the *Gaston Leroux.*

HOMEWORK

If only Victoria hadn't been so determined to impress her new science teacher, the problem might never have arisen.

She was feeling guilty about her happiness when she arrived home from school the day following Mr. Shelley's assumption of the biology class from Mrs. Polidori, whose ill health had finally forced her retirement. Victoria really didn't have anything major against Mrs. Polidori, but Mr. Shelley was an absolute dream.

"How was your day, dear?" Her mother called her usual greeting while Victoria struggled to fend off the affectionate attention of the family dog, an oversized mongrel named Percy.

"It was okay, Mom. We've got a new science teacher."

"That's nice." This was her mother's invariable reply, punctuation rather than communication.

"We're all supposed to paint our bodies and go to school naked Friday."

"That's nice. Make sure you do your homework right off."

Victoria nodded to herself, having confirmed that her mother was not, in fact, listening at all. But she remained in a good mood, even found a nice chewy for Percy before running upstairs to her room to work on this term's science project.

They'd been studying protozoa, and because this was Victoria's special interest, she'd been lightyears ahead of the other students and had found Mrs. Polidori's ponderous lectures boring and filled with minor factual errors. Percy followed her upstairs, but she determinedly closed the door so that he could not enter her private world of microscopes, chemicals, infrared lamps, and other, more arcane, instruments. The new nuclear accelerator her father had bought for her fourteenth birthday loomed large in one corner.

Without a second thought, she picked up the detailed cell diagrams she'd been working on and tossed them into the recycling field. Mrs. Polidori had taught physics last term, and Victoria still smarted from the woman's reaction to her functioning cold fusion generator. A "B minus" indeed!

For Mr. Shelley, however, something special was required. Victoria's brow furrowed as she quickly ran through a series of options, then uncreased as she made a decision. It was a good idea, but it would take time. She'd have to start right away to meet the Friday deadline.

The week passed quickly, but by Thursday Victoria knew that her experiment was not only successful, but had actually exceeded her original plan. Mr. Shelley would certainly be impressed.

Inside its glass tank, a genetically tailored amoeba had grown to a diameter of nearly half a meter, which was almost twice what she had expected. And judging by the spectroscopic analysis, the media was largely depleted of its nutritional content. She hastily corrected the situation, lest her experiment die prematurely.

In the morning, her father readily agreed to drive Victoria and her project to school. Once again, the nutrients had been leached from the solution, but she felt confident the creature would survive long enough to be graded.

At school, she borrowed a cart from the janitor and wheeled her project to the lab room, plugged its power cable into the wall, and hurried to home room. It was going to be a wonderful day.

It turned out otherwise.

Victoria arrived home that evening distracted and drained of enthusiasm.

"How was your day, dear?" Her mother seemed not to have moved from the couch for several days.

"Terrible. Disastrous. Horrible. Catastrophic. Worse than you could possibly imagine."

"That's nice."

Victoria dropped her books on the hall table and trudged up to her room, not reacting when Percy bounced along at her heels. She didn't even close the door, lay full length on the bed, and ignored Percy's energetic attempt to encourage petting. He was persistent, however, and she finally relented, scratching him gently behind the ears.

"Percy, you don't know how awful a day it's been. And I don't even have anyone to talk to about it."

Percy turned his head, ears alert, tongue hanging out of one side of his mouth.

"I know, Percy. You'd help me if you could. But you're just an animal. You wouldn't understand." Her shoulders rose and fell as she sighed dramatically, turned to stare at the far wall.

"There's just no way to explain to your dog how the homework ate the teacher."

THORACIC PARK

Chirr was polishing a freshly uncovered human skull when the ornithopter landed just outside the encampment, causing great consternation among the broodlings who were methodically clearing away soil from their latest find. Kachinka, his mate, clashed her mandibles angrily and made an obscene gesture with her antennae.

"Attend to the site," Chirr instructed. "I will deal with this."

He sank into haste posture and used all six legs to cover the intervening space, but even so the newcomer had already disembarked. "Professor Chirr? It's a pleasure to meet you, sir."

"What is the meaning of this intrusion?" Chirr rose to his full height and assumed the posture of outrage-verging-on-attack.

With a hasty, and rather superficial, adjustment to the stance of admission-of-error, the new arrival plunged on. "My name is Nakrok. I believe you've heard of me, though we've never met."

Indeed he had. Chirr slowly adjusted to reflect acceptance-of-apology while he considered the situation. Nakrok was the chief sponsor of this expedition, and had donated fully half of the broodlings currently scouring the area for artifacts.

"What can I do for you, Broodmaster Nakrok?" His body curled into mild-but-respectful deference.

"I know how important this project is to you, Professor, but I need your assistance urgently."

"My assistance?" Chirr switched to wary-cooperation.

"It will only be for a few days, I promise you, and your mate is welcome to come as well. I've made all the necessary arrangements, spared no expense."

The ornithopter dropped so suddenly into the wilderness preserve that Chirr and Kachinka immediately assumed preparedness-for-sudden-flight, even though there was no place to run to. Their wings were vestigial, ornamental rather than practical, the power of flight long since sacrificed in return for increased body weight and nerve tissue.

"Don't be alarmed," Nakrok reassured them. "We're just avoiding local turbulence."

Chirr's abdomen throbbed nervously and he picked up the

conversation to take his mind off the plummeting ornithopter.

"You say you've built some kind of theme part based on the ancient human culture?"

"Some kind of theme park, yes." Nakrok tried to suppress the tremor of triumph in his ventral lobes, but without much success. "But I'd much rather you wait to see it for yourself."

They were on the ground within moments, to Chirr's considerable relief, and disembarked into a waiting centivan. The driver fed his vehicle brush while they climbed aboard, and the two rows of articulated feet tapped restlessly against the ground.

"Rather remote, isn't it?" remarked Kachinka, who still resented being torn from her studies at the archaeological site.

"It's an unusual location, but worth the trouble." This time Nakrok's tremor was much more pronounced.

They rode in silence, Chirr and Kachinka enjoying the vivid scenery despite their mystification about the purpose of the trip. The steady beat of the centivan's legs was reassuring and Chirr was settling into a mini-estivation when he spotted something moving just beyond the trees to his right.

"Stop the van!"

The driver swiveled an eye stalk toward Nakrok, who signalled immediate-acquiescence. Kachinka glanced at her mate curiously but made no effort to follow when he stepped out of the vehicle. He moved only a few steps, fully upright, before catching sight of something so amazing that he momentarily lost control of his posture and sent a series of contradictory signals to his companions.

"That's a human being!" he said at last. "A living human being!"

Kachinka's head swiveled abruptly as she switched to suspicion-of-levity. Then she too spotted the pink creature picking berries from a clump of bushes just a few meters to one side of their route.

"Is it real or a construct?" Her voice betrayed the strain she felt.

"Oh, they're all quite real, I assure you. There are no illusions here."

"They?" Chirr turned to his host, slowly overcoming his confusion to assume respect-mixed-with-skeptical-reserve. "You have more than one of them?"

"Of course. Over a hundred in fact. So far."

"But...but how?"

"Let me tell you."

And tell them he did. DNA was fairly easy to come by because of the inexplicable human tendency to preserve their dead in sealed containers. There had even been some success cloning them, although without exception the living bodies that resulted were devoid of self awareness.

"You've heard of motigen, I assume?"

Chirr nodded. "It's the dynamic fluid manufactured by brain cells that determines which caste we join when we leave broodling stage."

"Well, we theorized that the same mechanism was present in the human species, that it quietly directed each individual into an appropriate cultural role, but that its ephemeral nature made the substance impossible to find under normal circumstances." Nakrok moved into imminent-revelation.

"But you found some anyway?" Kachinka prompted him, displaying curiosity-with-growing-impatience.

"That we did. Quite by accident, actually. One of my construction crews uncovered a buried installation that was still functional. It appears to have been some sort of nuclear powered cryogenic vault, and there were several hundred intact human bodies preserved inside. We think it was either a museum or some kind of strange religious cult. In any case, the important thing is that we found traces of motigen in most of the braincases."

"But surely it would have deteriorated with the passage of so much time. The human species has been extinct for thousands of brood cycles."

"None of the samples were undamaged, but by comparing what survived from one to another, we were able to run computer simulations that allowed us to extrapolate the missing data. We used surgical viruses to fill in the gaps and then began experimenting with bodies cloned from human DNA. Two years ago, we had our first success, and using accelerated growth techniques, we quickly populated the park. These," he gestured toward two browsing humans, "are primitive experiments whose motigen was flawed. They can do little more than forage. But our recent arrivals are much more advanced. The insurance salesman even seems to understand simple body postures and spoken language."

Chirr felt suddenly faint. "Insurance salesman? You have an insurance salesman?"

"Why, yes. We bred him right after the real estate agents. We plan a full range of attractions."

Chirr and Kachinka were lost in their own thoughts as their journey resumed, and they became aware of their surroundings again only when the centivan paused before the towering gates to the main park. Above them, the silhouette of a bare chested human figure had been painted onto the rightmost gate, both fists poised to pound a challenge on its obscenely hairy chest. On the opposite gate, a sign read simply: THORACIC PARK.

Chirr and Kachinka recovered some of their wits while being introduced to Grackl, whom Nakrok introduced as his game warden. "Grackl tells me when I'm taking foolish chances, you see. I have a tendency to get so involved with my work that I forget how dangerous these creatures are."

"They don't seem to move very quickly."

"No, the fastest ones are the lawyers, and then only when we give them an ambulance to chase."

Chirr was shocked. "Lawyers? You've bred lawyers?"

"Why certainly. They were one of the most common breeds after all."

"And the most dangerous."

"That adds to the park's atmosphere. But we're actually quite safe. Each section of the park is surrounded by thornfire bush. In fact, we had to give the roots a mild local anaesthetic in order to open the main gate. They're quite well contained."

"But what if something happened?" Kachinka switched to alarm-with-mild-accusation. "What if they got out? Their breeding capacity is enormous. That's what eventually destroyed them; they outran their food sources and their culture collapsed." Chirr's mandibles trembled at the very thought.

"No fear of that either. I assure you we've taken every precaution. The inhabitants of Thoracic Park are incapable of breeding. We've made sure of that."

"But how?" demanded Chirr. "Those two we saw on the way in. Didn't you say they were of different sexes?"

"Yes. But we've biologically altered them to prevent breeding. The humans were very much visually oriented in their sexual habits, you see, so we've made certain that they're all very ugly."

They met one more member of Nakrok's staff at the park headquarters, a surly, overweight individual named Frell whose every posture included at least a hint of impatience-with-trifles.

"Frell is unhappy with me," Nakrok admitted later. "He's a contract botanist I hired to oversee the thornfire planting, and I'm afraid he underestimated the acidity of the soil. But a contract is a contract. He's spun his web and now he'll have to sleep in it."

"You said you had some kind of automated tour set up for us?"

"Yes, indeed. We're just waiting for the others. Ahh, here they are now!"

Chirr shifted to growing-unease-and-anticipation-of-distress when he saw the broodlings emerge from a nearby building. Fully six score of them, all exuding the same clan pheromone as did Nakrok himself.

"This is my most recent brood. They'll be accompanying you on the tour."

Chirr felt his posture shifting more definitely toward distress but Kachinka touched her antennae to his. "Steady. You can put up with them for a short time."

He supposed she was right, but he didn't have to like it.

The tour was not a great success. The real estate agents too busy drawing lines in the soil and arguing with each to pay attention to the tour van. The night watchmen were nocturnal and currently asleep, the accountant sat with his back to them, slowly moving stones from one pile to another, and the hairdresser was sick and sedated.

Then they reached the exterminator's compound. Chirr and Kachinka peered through the ropes of thornfire bush but the dreaded creature, a monster whose name was used by broodmasters to frighten broodlings into behaving themselves, was nowhere to be seen. Chirr would have welcomed its presence for more than professional reasons. Nakrok's broodlings were full of nervous energy, kept running across the ceiling of the van as well as the aisles, and were generally making nuisances of themselves. A little scare might help keep them in line.

If he'd known what was happening back at park headquarters, he might have altered his wish.

Frell assumed acceptance-under-protest and ended his interview with Nakrok, even though the posture had not reflected his true feelings. It was clear that the broodmaster would not agree to compensate him for the extra expenses he had incurred, and that in the ordinary course of events he would be compelled to dismember himself to appease his creditors. But Frell had a contingency plan.

He returned to his workroom and retrieved the vial concealed in an innocent bottle of mandibular cream, then filled a syringe and walked out onto the grounds. The nearest thornfire bush was only a few meters away. With a quick look around to make certain he was unobserved, Frell injected a contagious virus into the largest strand of thornbush within reach.

Within an hour, the entire thornfire containment system would be rendered temporarily inert. Frell already had samples of various strains of motigen concealed in his egg sacs. Once he reached the mainland, he'd sell them to one of Nakrok's rivals.

Unfortunately, Frell didn't know that his virus also affected the centivans. He would learn the truth shortly, when his stolen vehicle fell into a coma and left him at the mercy of a hungry laundromat attendant.

Chirr was too preoccupied to notice the first irregularity in the centivan's movement, but Kachinka picked it up right away.

"Something's wrong with our vehicle," she said quietly.

Sure enough, they were jolted almost immediately as a half dozen legs folded and collapsed on one side. The remaining ones thrashed for a few more seconds before falling silent as well. The broodlings began to screech, some annoyed, some frightened.

"Is it dead?"

"I don't think so." Kachinka inclined her antennae toward a set of exposed ventricles. "It's still breathing."

"What do you supposed happened?"

She curled into the posture of confusion-and-mild-concern. "I suppose it might be sick."

Chirr was about to make an intemperate remark when one of the broodlings swarmed up his body and clammered for attention, gesturing with one arm toward the containment line.

Something was struggling to emerge from the thornfire bush.

"That's impossible!" Chirr's whispered protest was loud enough to send the broodlings into another furious race up and down the inner walls of their vehicle.

But there was no question that the human exterminator was making its way steadily forward through the barrier, brushing the thornfire barbs aside with frightening ease.

"We can't wait for this thing to wake up," he said quietly. "We're going to have to make a run for it."

Kachinka glanced meaningfully at the horde of broodlings swarming around them.

"Yes, I know. But we don't have any choice."

"All of them?" Nakrok glared at the biotechnician. "Are you saying they're all inactive?"

"Yes, sir." The technician didn't look happy. "Somehow they've been contaminated with a contagious neuro-agent. There are several strains of virus that would have this effect. Frell's an expert on viruses. I'm sure he can find a counteragent as soon as we've located him."

Grackl entered the room at that moment, assumed the posture of frustrated-lack-of-success. "He's nowhere within the headquarters area, and one of the centivans is missing."

Nakrok's mandibles clenched with anger. "Well we'll have to make do without him then. You!" He pointed directly at the technician. "Isn't there a general serum we can use to get the thornfires back on line?"

But before he could answer, one of Grackl's staff burst into the room with more bad news. "The lawyers have broken out of their pen!"

Grackl twisted into extreme-rage-with-overtones-of fear. "If they escape into the main park, we'll never catch them. They're the cleverest of the lot."

"They're not headed for the park. Noctor saw them breaking into the library."

"The library?" Grackl turned to Nakrok, who slowly curled into admitted-lack-of-answer.

Chirr and Kachinka led the broodlings into a small cavern for the night. "Don't worry," she reassured the young ones. "They're modified tree dwellers and won't come down after us." She felt less confident than she sounded.

"What do you suppose happened?" Chirr was still shaking from the exertions of the day. They'd evaded the exterminator with some difficulty, encountered what appeared to be an immature butler dusting the leaves in a fern grove, and were briefly chased by a pair of letter carriers before eluding them in a swamp.

"I have no idea. The park security system must have malfunctioned. I'm sure they have parties out looking for us, but the park is so big, I think we'll have to make our way back on our own."

And so they did, over the course of the next day, arriving in sight of the headquarters compound just as the sun was starting to drop behind the nearby mountains.

"Everything looks quiet," Kachinka observed quietly. They were crouched on a knoll, staring down into the cluster of buildings.

"Too quiet. Where is everybody?"

"Out looking for us?"

In the cramped space, it was difficult to assume skepticism-with-hope so Chirr compromised on uncertainty-with-anticipation.

"Well, we can't wait here. Let's go."

Chirr led, followed by a double column of broodlings, with Kachinka following to make sure none of the young ones strayed. They crossed the cultivated grounds without incident, reached the entrance to the main hall.

"I'll take them inside," Kachinka offered. "You find out where everybody is."

Chirr inclined into acceptance-of-suggestion and waited only long enough to assure himself that the last of the broodlings was accounted for before proceeding.

The estivation room was empty, the feeding hives abandoned, the centivan nest quiet. Chirr passed them by and headed for the park control room, convinced that it would be occupied even if everyone else had been evacuated.

Grackl hailed him as he approached, rushing out into the open to embrace Chirr with intertwined antennae. "You've survived! And the others?"

Chirr explained quickly. "What happened?"

Grackl shifted rapidly through a number of postures, conveying confusion, anger, fear, uncertainty, and a host of other unpleasant emotional states.

"The thornbush was deactivated. We've just managed to get an antidote flushed through the system."

Chirr allowed himself to relax slightly. "Then the humans are back under control?"

"Most of them." Grackl turned an eyestalk toward the control building. "But the lawyers escaped and got into the library. They barricaded the doors, killed and ate poor Skrezzle, and it was pure luck that we were able to surround the place with revived thornfire before they broke out."

"But they're confined again, aren't they? So why do you appear so distraught?"

Grackl's body slumped into resigned-to-disaster. "They're smart, you know, smarter than we thought. All this time we've been studying them, they've been studying us as well. It seems they've picked up enough of our language to use the library, and they spent the last day reading."

"So what? They're just animals, aren't they? It's not as if they can understand what they read."

"That's just it. They discovered an obscure law under which they are legally an endangered species, and by the provisions of that law, we can no longer confine them to a prescribed habitat. We have to let them go free." He assumed the posture of concern-mixed-with-relief. "At least they won't be able to breed."

In a remote part of Thoracic Park, two ugly faced humans closed their eyes and made love.

ARTIFACTS OF ART

It is an unfortunate fact of history that many truly wonderful artists are never recognized during their lifetimes, but in the case of Terence Stoddard, this oversight had repercussions of unusual magnitude.

Born in the small town of Managansett, Rhode Island, the only child of Bert and Ernestine Stoddard, Terence distinguished himself early in life by drawing caricatures of his classmates that demonstrated a truly remarkable eye not only for detail but for the essence of the human character. Unfortunately, a less than kind portrayal of his second grade teacher, Ruth Glancy, was so widely circulated that it inevitably was brought to her attention. The elder Stoddards were summoned to the principal's office and young Terence was sternly ordered to curb his artistic inclinations.

His urge to draw proved irrepressible, however, and some of his classmates recalled in their later years the elaborate embellishments he added to otherwise uninspired graffiti in the boys' rooms scattered throughout Managansett Elementary and later, at Sheffield Junior High. Stoddard was forced to repeat several grades despite evaluations from teachers and guidance counselors which described him as being above average in intelligence and even gifted in creativity and the ability to channel his imagination into constructive work. The difficulty was the appended comments describing him as "unwilling or unable to apply himself" to the course material as required; he was chronically inattentive in class, failed to complete outside work on schedule, and performed poorly on tests, although there survives enough anecdotal and other data to indicate that he did in fact retain a considerable portion of the subject matter to which he was exposed.

Stoddard, quite simply, couldn't have cared less about his schoolwork.

The observations of his peers are surprisingly consistent, considering the lack of sophistication they possessed when they knew him and the considerable passage of years before they were asked to recall their memories of Terence Stoddard. He left school in 1990, on his sixteenth birthday in fact, halfway through what would have been his second attempt to complete his freshman year of high school. Both of his parents died less than two years later, victims of an automobile accident, and the proceeds of their insurance were sufficient to support Stoddard until early in 2001.

What little we know about Stoddard's remarkable accomplishments during that decade has been derived inferentially. He lived a reclusive life, rarely leaving the small house on Whippoorwill Street where he'd been raised. What is quite certain is that he spent a large portion of that time painting. An examination of relevant financial records reveals that fully a third of his expenditures went to pay for paints, canvases, frames, and other supplies, and there is evidence as well that he dabbled in sculpture, although no examples of this work have survived. It is assumed that he was dissatisfied with the results and destroyed them, as seems to have been the fate of many of his paintings, fragments of which have been found during the excavation of the Whippoorwill Street basement.

With the freedom to paint unmolested, and fired with the enthusiasm of youth, Stoddard produced most of his enduring masterpieces during this period, including *Black Velvet Child with Lurid Eyes, Woman with Three Arms, Self Portrait with Lemons*, and *Sanitation Squad on Noah's Ark*. Stoddard also maintained a meticulously catalogued collection of sketches, which filled eight filing cabinet drawers at the time of their discovery, but most of these were subsequently destroyed during the Boston Insurrection of 2040 and only photocopies have survived.

During the fall of 2010, Stoddard apparently began to realize that the funds he'd inherited were not inexhaustible. Indeed, an examination of his financial transactions indicates that he would probably have depleted his bank account by early the following year. He applied for minimal employment under the Universal Sustenance Act of 2007, and his scores on a battery of aptitude, psychological, and performance tests are a matter of public record.

Two months later, Stoddard was offered and accepted a position working in the Facilities Maintenance Department of the state of Rhode Island. Although he was to hold this position until his death in 2026, he was never offered a promotion and insofar as art historians have been able to ascertain, he never made an effort to find alternate employment. Performance evaluations invariably characterized his work as adequate but lackluster.

When Stoddard died of Twonk's Disease in June of 2026, he left no will and no heirs. Under the provisions of the newly enacted Directed Probate Laws, title to his estate passed to the state legislature after thirty days without a valid claimant, and what followed might well have been a major tragedy for the art world. Fortunately, Tracie Shotwell was assigned to oversee the liquidation of the house and its assets, and she possessed the wit to recognize that the several hundred canvasses stored in the house were evidence of a major, undiscovered talent.

The details of what followed are so well known that there is no point in discussing them in detail here. Shotwell convinced her supervisor that the find merited the attention of a professional art expert. Within a month, reproductions of some of the more remarkable works were to be found in such publications as *Playperson, Artweek*, and *What's Happening!* State authorities knew a good thing when they saw it and, faced with a major budget shortfall, began auctioning the paintings in limited quantities, a process which continued for nearly two years resulting in the first significant 21st Century cash surplus for any state except Cuba.

That might have been the end of it had it not been for the actions of a determined art collector named Alex Saroda. Saroda was arguably Stoddard's most ardent admirer, had in fact expended much of his personal fortune to acquire no less than twenty six of the original paintings. He also managed to purchase a half dozen sketches before the rest were auctioned off in one lot to the Boston Museum of Contemporary Art. His obsession was so great that he successfully bid for the house on Whippoorwill Street after learning that Stoddard had repainted the interior walls himself.

That was where the trouble started.

Saroda decided to write an exhaustive biography of his idol, and as part of his research, he accessed Stoddard's employment records. By cross referencing these with the Facilities Maintenance Department's project database, he was able to develop a list of the sites and assignments in which the artist had been involved. To his delight, he discovered that Stoddard had frequently been employed as a painter, refurbishing state property, both interiors and exteriors, producing road signs, and even operating the equipment which applied a clear white solid or dotted line to the center of highways using the new, permanent elastomers.

Terence Stoddard: Pragmatic Art appeared in 2027. Among the supplementary material in the book was a complete index to all rooms, buildings, artifacts, and sections of highway which had been painted in total or in part by Stoddard, with notations indicating which had yet to be redone.

Within a week of its publication, the damage was already evident. Art collecting had become the major national pastime by 2020, outdistancing baseball, hoopglimming, computer bulletin boards, and -- just possibly - sex. Avid fans of Stoddard's work descended on the Water Department, the section of Highway between Managansett and Scituate, the Keller-Blake Condominium Complex, the Anderson Bridge, and elsewhere, snarling traffic, interrupting the flow of business, and causing general chaos. The state hastily tried to swell its coffers further by charging admission, but angry crowds overturned ticket booths in several locations and Governor Heramia finally announced that "as a service to the art loving citizenry", all Stoddard sites would be freely open to the public, although the flow of traffic would henceforth be regulated to promote order.

Then the thefts began. Traffic control signs, highway exit warnings, and other easily portable objects believed to have been painted by Stoddard began to disappear. Although in some cases, his authorship had been authenticated, in many others his involvement was dubious at best, and there arose almost immediately an underground black market in forged Stoddard "Stop" signs, or example, which moved a total number of counterfeit works that are estimated to have exceeded the number of street corner locations in the entire city of Providence and its suburbs.

In response, the state began issuing non-reproducible holographs of authenticity and affixing them only to those surviving works which had been proven beyond reasonable doubt to have been painted at least in large measure by Terence Stoddard. The condition of some of these had begun to deteriorate, and in fact a work crew was just about to lay a fresh coat of paint over the Anderson Bridge guardrail when they were set upon by a crowd of art fans who physically restrained them until the work order was revoked.

The crisis reached its height in the spring of 2028, when a twenty foot strip of asphalt running down the center of Treadfast Street disappeared sometime between midnight and dawn on April 24. The purloined roadway was one of the few proven to be Stoddard's handiwork and a holographic plaque embedded in the surface was removed as well. When news of the theft became public knowledge, there was a flurry of similar incidents. Clapboards and siding were stolen from state and municipal buildings, more sections of pavement were torn up and carried off, someone used an acetylene torch to remove a twelve foot section of railing from the Anderson Bridge, and there were similar incidents involving statues, interior walls, and city vehicles, including the disappearance of a relatively new Boeing Earthmover.

And as usual, many of the items stolen or defaced had never been touched by Terence Stoddard, or if they had, his original painting had subsequently been covered over.

Fortunately, by late spring, Samantha Brach's theory of "Re-Found Art" gained wide popularity and the public fascination with Terence Stoddard declined. Rhode Island was subsequently the first, but not last, state to pass an Artistic Integrity Law, ostensibly to protect the reputation of talented artisans but actually designed to prevent similar problems from arising in the future.

The next major crisis to convulse the art world came in 2029 with the publication of Tramwell's "Thesis of Fecal Art". Tramwellists, chanting their war cry "Art should stink!", first made their appearance...

--- Excerpted from Velcro and Naugahyde's *History of Confrontational Art*, Muse House, Seattle, 2049.

NO PROBLEM

I swear I had good intentions. I know that sounds pretty weak, but it's the truth. Look, I'll tell it the way it happened and you can judge for yourself.

My name in Herbert Franken and I've been working toward a masters degree in biochemistry at Brown University for the past year. My parents wanted me to go into the family business, but I don't even like pizza and I wanted more for myself than a life sweating over pepperoni and tomato sauce. When the oven exploded and killed them both, as well as burning down the restaurant, I took it as a sign that I'd made the right choice.

Brown allocated space for its grad students in the laboratory building, but it was hard to concentrate there with people coming and going all the time. No problem. The insurance had left me pretty well off, so I decided to clean out part of the basement and put together my own facility. I was working on monitoring rates of cell degeneration, so I didn't really need a lot of room.

That meant going through all of the boxes and crates and trunks of family memorabilia that my parents had stored there, most of which they hadn't even looked at after shipping them all the way here from Europe. Some of it I threw out, and most of the rest went to a storage locker. The only thing I kept at the house in Managansett was a crate full of old journals that looked like family histories.

It cost more than I expected to outfit my laboratory, even buying used equipment where possible, but it only took a few weeks to get everything delivered and installed to my liking. The only drawback was the ventilation. There were two tiny basement windows, but they didn't provide much circulation. No problem. By opening the bulkhead door that led up into the backyard I even had a refreshing breeze.

So now I guess I should tell you about Mrs. Williams. Gretchen Williams was my neighbor, an elderly retired nurse who had lived in the small cottage next door for as long as I could remember. She had to be at least seventy, but it might have been a lot more than that. Her skin was dark and wrinkled like the dried fruit you find in trail mix. My dad used to call her the "neighborhood inspector" because she walked up and down the streets every once in a while with a pencil and pad, looking for code violations she could report to the town hall – broken windows, visible garbage cans, peeling paint, things like that. Once when I was a kid, she caught a whiff of some concoction I'd cooked up with my chemistry set and came over to complain, and on another occasion she walked right into our house, demanding to know when Dad was going to trim the front hedge. She was an incredibly nosy woman, asked all sorts of personal questions, and either didn't realize how unpopular she was or just didn't care.

My parents had never talked much about our family back in Germany and I always suspected that they were involved with the Nazis or worked in a concentration camp or something like that. I remember one time Dad let something slip about the family castle, but he insisted he was joking and got mad when I pushed so I let it go. The journals were likely to answer at least some of my questions. Once my first experiments were underway, I had to spend a lot of time waiting for dead organic matter to get even deader, so I pulled one of them out and started reading. They were in German, naturally. No problem. I'd grown up speaking German at home and English everywhere else.

They were pretty dull, actually, at least until I found my multiply-great-grandfather's oversized, brass bound account of his experiments. The name inscribed inside the cover was a bit of a shock. Viktor Frankenstein. I thought it must be some kind of elaborate joke, but there was no question about the age of the journals, and when I read through the first few pages, I felt a flicker of excitement. His observations were crude by contemporary standards, but there were hints of an acute intelligence and an almost supernatural insight into the processes of life. I was struck by some coincidental similarities with my own work, and read on far into the night.

The next morning, I threw out the cultures I'd started, ordered some new equipment, and began rearranging the lab.

Please don't get the impression that I had suddenly turned into some kind of mad scientist. I had no intention of digging up dead bodies at midnight, erecting a lightning rod on my roof, or stealing brains from Brown University. Nor were there any hints of such madness in the journal. The experiments described there were limited to rats and other lab animals. Contrary to the story promulgated by Mary Shelley, who may have known my ancestor socially, there was no suggestion that Viktor ever experimented on human subjects. At least not in the journals in my possession, which ended abruptly in 1816.

With modern equipment, I was able to duplicate and improve on Viktor's work in a matter of weeks. I quickly confirmed what the journals had already suggested. The process could indeed generate vitality from dead cells, but there was no possibility of restoring the higher functions except on the most rudimentary level. A dead mouse's heart might resume its pumping, the tiny form might even stand and walk about and even go through the motions of eating or drinking, but it might just as easily begin gnawing on its own tail. Even among lower animals, the mind is more than just the physical structure of the brain.

One Saturday morning, I found Mrs. Williams' cat in my yard, chewing on a dead sparrow. After chasing the cat back over the fence, I examined the tiny corpse which appeared completely undamaged, other than the missing head. I couldn't resist the temptation, injected some of my serum into the cooling body, and was immediately rewarded by a slight fluttering of the wings. I hadn't anticipated the possible consequences, however, and I wasn't quick enough when it suddenly rose into the air and began flying around the basement. Its movements were random and had I thought to close the bulkhead door, I could have captured it in short order. Unfortunately, it blundered through the opening and quickly vanished. The stimulating effects of the treatment would wear off after a few hours so presumably no harm was done.

A few days later I was preparing a new experiment when Mrs. Williams came boldly down the cement steps, demanding to know what I was doing. "I open the kitchen window this morning and what a stink! I thought something must have died over here." Her appearance was so unexpected that I didn't react until she was halfway across the basement. "What's this stuff then? Are you making drugs down here?" She looked at the lab equipment suspiciously. "I'll bet the police would be interested to know about this, young man."

I stood up and advanced on her immediately, angry at the intrusion and concerned that she might damage something. "This is private property, Mrs. Williams. You have no right to come in here."

"Got something to hide then, do you?" She reached out toward my spectrometer and I caught her wrist reflexively. "How dare you!" Her face twisted in outrage. "How dare you lay hands on me!"

"Please get out of my house or I will call the police." My voice trembled. I felt like a child again, terrified of adult authority. I had never had the courage to so much as set foot on Mrs. Williams' property. For years I had been convinced that she was a witch, and that irrational fear quickened my pulse.

"Call them then! I'd like to see you explain all of this!" And she reached toward the bubbling vials where I was brewing a fresh batch of the revitalization serum.

I only meant to push her away, but she was a tiny woman and I'm not a small man. She lost her balance and fell over so quickly that she never even cried out. I heard the solid thud as her head struck the cement wall and I knew she was dead at that instant.

No, I didn't think that I could bring her back to life and send her home. Not exactly anyway. What I did next was a product of panic and guilt. It had been an accident, certainly, and she had been trespassing as well. But I'm six feet tall, two hundred pounds and here I was contemplating explaining to the police how an elderly one hundred pound woman received a fatal head wound in my basement. It would be inconvenient and embarrassing at best, possibly much worse. So I considered my options and came up with a plan.

No problem. I had plenty of serum. I lifted her onto the bench and half emptied a freshly filled hypodermic into her body. The results, if any, would be apparent within minutes. I have to confess that, despite everything, I was curious to see what would happen.

There was no thunderstorm, the lights didn't flicker, and I neither cackled nor rubbed my hands together in sinister fashion. I simply waited until the serum had had time to infuse the tissues. Although I tried to remain calm and collected, I have to admit that it gave me rather a start when she abruptly sat up on the bench.

To outward appearances, she appeared completely normal. Even the soft spot on the side of her head was hidden by her hair, and the small trickle of blood had completely dried. I couldn't help apologizing as I took her by the elbows and lifted her down from the table. She was a bit unsteady at first, but she followed docilely as I led her up the steps and out into the open. Her eyes were focused but I sensed no intelligence behind them. My earlier experiments had suggested that certain behavioral patterns remained intact, but no more. The sparrow had sought to escape into the open, crickets scurried toward dark corners, and one of the white rats had even remembered how to operate the feeding lever, then ignored the food pellet that dropped into the dish.

My plan was simple. I planned to take her back to her house and close her up inside, then call the police and tell them that I'd found her lying in her backyard, had assisted her into the house, but was concerned that she'd suffered a concussion. Which, of course, she had. No problem.

I even had a stroke of luck. Gus Robinson was watering his grass across the street. I waved when he glanced in our direction, and he nodded casually. I led Mrs. Williams, or her body anyway, up the porch steps, opened the screen door, and gently pushed her through. She advanced a few steps, then stopped. I waited, but she didn't move, so I let the door close and turned away.

Gus was coiling up the hose when I reached him. "Morning, Gus."

He raised his eyebrows. I guess I'm not the sociable type and it kind of surprised him that I'd initiated a conversation. "Morning, Herbert. What's the old biddy up to today?" He glanced at Mrs. Williams' house. He hadn't spoken to her since the day she reported him for putting up a flagpole that violated a town ordinance.

"She tripped over something and hit her head. I saw her lying in the garden and helped her inside. I'm wondering if I should call an ambulance or something. She might have a concussion."

"Her head's too hard for that."

I tried to smile but it felt wrong. "Even so, I feel funny about not calling someone. I don't think she has any family in the area."

"Drove them all to suicide, most likely." Gus finished with the hose and took a tentative step toward his front door, as though he wasn't sure the conversation was over.

I decided not to push too far. "Maybe I'll just check on her later."

I waited for an hour, then went through the motions. I looked in through the screen door, but she was nowhere in sight. I rang the bell and then called her name, hoping one of the neighbors would hear me, then went back to my house and called the police, told them my version of the situation somewhat apologetically. A cruiser showed up ten minutes later and a uniformed officer rang the bell, rapped on the door, walked around peering in through the windows. I waited until he'd been at it for a few minutes then went out and introduced myself.

"Is there anyone else living here?" he asked.

I shook my head. "Just Mrs. Williams. That's why I was so concerned." Something moved in the air at the periphery of my vision, a small dark blur. I glanced up to see a bird, or at least most of one, flutter past and slam into the trunk of Mrs. Williams' birch tree. "She didn't look good," I said hastily as Officer Tremblay's head began to turn. The bird, still twitching, fell out of sight.

He tried calling again, then opened the screen door. "Please wait out here, sir," he said firmly. I stood on the porch, shifting my weight nervously from foot to foot, rehearsing my lines over and over again. He seemed to take an awfully long time, but eventually he came back outside and shut the door.

"There's no one home."

Well, you can imagine how startled I was. "She has to be there," I insisted, perhaps a bit too strongly. "Maybe she wandered into a closet or something."

He shook his head. "It's a very small house, Mr. Franken, and I looked everywhere. She's not home. Maybe she took herself off to see a doctor, or felt well enough to go shopping. I don't see a car." He glanced toward the driveway.

"She doesn't drive."

"Then maybe she asked someone to drive her or called a taxi."

I knew how impossible that was, but I couldn't very well say anything. "I guess you're right, officer. I'm sorry if I wasted your time."

"That's all right, sir. Better safe than sorry."

I probably should have left it at that. Mrs. Williams, or her body at least, would turn up eventually. But I had to know what had happened to her. Somewhere, deep in the recesses of my mind, was the sudden fear that she hadn't been dead after all, that she'd recovered her wits and would tell someone what I'd done to her. The blow to the head I could explain, but how could I justify injecting strange substances into her body? No, I couldn't rest until I knew what had happened.

She couldn't have gotten far, not without help, so I set out to find her, methodically working my way around each separate block. I saw a few people outside, and I even ventured to ask some of them whether they'd seen an elderly woman wandering about, but no one could be helpful. I was almost ready to give up and go home when I turned onto Burkett Street and heard the hammering.

I need to tell you about Bert Sanderson. Bert was Mrs. Williams' nemesis. She'd complained that his dog was barking so many times that the animal control officer finally threatened legal action. Bert had been so enraged that he'd assaulted the officer, and was lucky to have gotten a suspended sentence and a hefty fine A weeks later he had been caught throwing eggs at Mrs. Williams' windows one night after a few too many beers, and she'd pressed charges which had been added to resisting arrest and another assault charge. Bert spent six months in prison and lost his job. There had been a few more incidents of vandalism since his release – someone had twice sprayed her garden with weed killer – but Bert had not been proven responsible, and the truth was, Mrs. Williams had made a lot of enemies.

Although I only knew Bert casually, I'd heard that their latest run-in had involved the utility shed he'd built in his backyard. Apparently it was three inches taller than allowed by town ordinances, and Mrs. Williams had objected when he'd applied for a variance. The last I'd heard, he had removed the roof and was remodeling. I had almost passed his property when the hammering stopped and I heard him shouting angrily.

"Get out of here, you senile bitch, or I swear I'll use the hose on you!"

I knew who it had to be and started in that direction. As I passed the corner of the house, I saw Mrs. Williams standing near the unfinished shed while Bert stalked toward the garden hose that lay in the grass near his stockade fence. I hesitated, trying to decide how to proceed, never guessing that I'd just lost my chance to prevent a tragedy.

Mrs. Williams stooped to the bright red toolbox at her feet and picked up a claw headed hammer. I was momentarily paralyzed with astonishment because it had seemed such a purposeful act that my earlier fear, that she wasn't dead after all, came back full force. Then she was moving and her arm was going up and I realized what she intended and started after her but of course it was too late. She hit him from behind and I didn't think she could have exerted enough force to do much damage, but Bert slumped forward on his face with a grunt. He wasn't moving.

When I reached his side a second later, he wasn't breathing either.

Mrs. Williams was just standing there, her face neutral, and she didn't resist when I took the hammer from her hand. Then I realized my mistake, took out my handkerchief, and wiped the handle to remove my fingerprints. "Mrs. Williams?" I asked, barely above a whisper. She didn't answer, didn't even seem to hear me.

I thought about taking her away and returning to my original plan. I could tell the police I'd spotted her while out for a walk. But Bert complicated things. His death was obviously no accident. I didn't think anyone had seen me there, but I couldn't be certain. For a minute or two I stood, unable to think clearly, and then the sound of children shouting somewhere close by made me panic. The back door to Bert's house was unlocked and he lived alone. I took Mrs. Williams by the elbow and brought her inside, shut her in the bathroom. Then I carried Bert in through the kitchen to the garage. His station wagon was there and a few minutes of searching turned up his keys. I bundled his inert body into the back and covered it with a blanket.

I wasn't thinking clearly, obviously, but I wanted to buy some time. Bert's wife would be home from work in another hour or two and I didn't want her, or anyone else, to find the body until I had a plan. I collected Mrs. Williams', who was perfectly docile now, and put her in the back seat. It was taking a chance to drive Bert's car but I hoped to have it out of sight before anyone took particular notice. Five minutes later it was inside my garage, and I had closed the curtains on the windows so that no one could look in and see it. No problem.

I went inside to look for some clothesline, intending to restrain Mrs. Williams, but before I could find any, the doorbell rang. It was Gus Robinson, who wanted to tell me that a squad car had stopped by looking for me.

"Why are they looking for me?" My voice trembled.

Gus shrugged. "He didn't say, just asked me to tell you that he'd stop back later." Gus seemed to want to talk, maybe hoping I was privy to some delicious secret, and I didn't want to make him suspicious by being too anxious to have him leave, so it took another couple of minutes to get rid of him. Even so I was forced to be rather abrupt, and there was an odd look on his face when he left. I found the clothes line and went out to the garage.

Mrs. Williams was gone.

I ran quickly from room to room, and noticed that the patio doors were open. I was sure I had closed them so I went outside, resisting the temptation to call her name. She wasn't likely to respond to it, anyway, and someone might hear me. I ran around to the side yard, slowed when I saw Gus across the street. I didn't think he'd seen me so I retreated around the corner of the house quickly. Then I went next door, climbing the fence so I couldn't be spotted, and searched the cottage. There was no sign of Mrs. Willliams.

I went back inside, telling myself that it wasn't a problem. If she was gone, I could just revert to my original plan. She'd collapse in a few hours anyway and there was nothing to connect me with her death. Bert was a separate problem. As soon as it was dark, I could drive the car to Breakneck Hill, prop him behind the wheel, and send him over one of the drop-offs, then set fire to the wreck. It would be a long walk back, but I could stay in the woods for most of that distance. No one would be likely to see me there. No problem.

Once I'd decided on a plan, I felt better, but then I started to worry again. What about rigor mortis? What if the body was so stiff that I couldn't get it into position?. Maybe I should prop it up in the passenger seat now. I started for the garage.

And heard something move.

Was it possible that Bert hadn't been killed after all? I opened the door to the garage with my heart in my throat, then felt a mixture of relief and shock. It wasn't Bert who was moving; it was Mrs. Williams. Somehow I'd missed her, and she'd come back. She was standing at the rear of the station wagon, staring down through the open rear window at Bert's inert body. I walked around to stand beside her, already working on a new scenario.

Something glittered in her right hand. It was a hypodermic needle. One of mine. In fact, it was the same one I'd used to inject her with serum. I'd only used half but it was almost empty now.

Bert rolled over and sat up.

My chest began to hurt and I realized that I was laughing, great gasping sobs of laughter. I forced myself to calm down. Bert's body seemed content to remain where it was, so I turned to Mrs. Williams, relieved her of the hypodermic, and led her away. She didn't struggle while I tied her to the tool bench. I would have to find some way of restraining Bert next, but I'd barely begun to consider that problem when the doorbell rang again. I went into the house, closing the door behind me.

It was Officer Tremblay again. "Would you mind if I came in a moment, sir?"

I offered him a seat, which he politely refused. "I'm following up on your neighbor, Mrs. Williams. You haven't seen her since your first report, have you?"

"No," I lied.

"Well, we've had a call from a Mrs. Pereira a couple of blocks from here. She said an elderly woman who fits the description walked past her house about two hours ago. She said the woman had blood on her face and seemed dazed. If she'd called in at the time, we might have been able to find her, but she kept quiet until her conscience started to bother her. We just wanted to make sure that we're not looking for two separate women." He read a description of Mrs. Sanderson's clothing from his notebook and I confirmed that she'd been dressed identically when I'd last seen her.

"Thank you for your assistance, Mr. Franken."

"I just hope it helps," I said with mock sincerity. Officer Tremblay turned toward the door and I started forward to open it.

There was a loud thump from the garage. We both heard it, but I pretended not to. "Are you alone here, Mr. Franken?"

"Yes, I am officer. Something must have fallen over. It's nothing to worry about."

"I'm sure that's the case, but I was wondering if it might be the missing lady wandering again."

"The garage door is locked." Something in my manner must have betrayed me because he was immediately suspicious.

"Would you mind if I had a look, sir?"

I searched for a rational reason to object, but Tremblay didn't wait for one. He started toward the kitchen and I was forced to trail along in his wake. My heart sunk and I knew this was the end. He'd see Mrs. Williams as soon as he stepped into the garage.

He wasted no time and I saw the way his head snapped up as the door opened. His hand was dropping to his weapon as he spun around to face me. "Please raise your hands, Mr. Franken."

I slowly began to do as I was told, but I never completed the movement. A crowbar flashed through the air, bouncing off his skull, and Officer Tremblay dropped like a stone. It was Bert, of course. Even dead, he hated the police with a passion. The crowbar rose and fell twice more before I ran forward and took it away from Bert. By then Mrs. Williams had untied herself as well and she was staggering around the garage, apparently trying to stab Bert with the hypodermic, which she'd retrieved from the shelf where I'd put it.

So there I was with three dead bodies, two of them still moving around, and two cars to dispose of them, one a police cruiser. I sat down for a while to think things through and decided that the first priority was to get rid of the cruiser. I couldn't carry Officer Tremblay's body down to it in the daylight, so I'd have to dispose of that separately. No problem. Bert was still wandering around, so I found some more clothes line and tied him to one end of the bench. He didn't seem to mind. By then Mrs. Williams was stabbing the dead policeman over and over with the empty hypodermic. I took it out of her hand and she sat down heavily. The serum was obviously starting to wear off.

I was just catching my breath when the doorbell rang. It was Gus from across the street.

"Hi. I saw the cop car out front and wondered if there'd been any news about Mrs. Williams."

I didn't invite him in. The noises from the garage had stopped, but I had a dead policeman and two animated corpses to deal with. It wasn't an appropriate time for entertaining.

I opened my mouth, intending to tell him that there'd been no news, that Tremblay was using the bathroom, and it wasn't a good time, but before I could open my mouth, his eyes widened and he looked past me. "Mrs. Williams! We were all worried about you."

Somehow she'd found the strength to come into the house. I was paralyzed with indecision, and of course Gus decided to brush past me.

She didn't like Gus particularly either, so she stabbed him with the hypodermic. He gave a surprised little cry, dropped to his knees, and fell headlong. There was no more serum, so at least he wasn't likely to get up any time soon. I decided to consider that my luck had finally changed for the better.

Mrs. Williams had collapsed by the time I had finished dragging Gus into the garage. Officer Tremblay was moving around a little; apparently there'd been enough of the serum left to cause some reaction, but he couldn't stand up. He was pawing at his weapon and I took it away from him just to be safe. I carried Mrs. Williams out next. She barely moved so that was no problem.

It was later than I had realized. The day had gotten away from me. As soon as it was fully dark, I was going to carry the bodies next door, then move Bert's car out onto the street. I'd set fire to the house, wait until it was going pretty well, then call in the alarm. Let the police interpret the four bodies however they wanted after that.

By the time I was willing to risk it, Mrs. Williams was completely still, and the other two were obviously winding down. Tremblay was still pawing at his holster but he couldn't stand up, so I ended up carrying all four of them, one at a time. Then I went down to the basement and arranged some rags and other combustibles near the oil tank. It was harder to get the fire going than I expected, but eventually I was satisfied.

I decided to have one last look around upstairs before leaving and that was my last mistake. When I stepped through the doorway into the kitchen, I felt something brush against my leg. There was a click and I looked down just in time to see Officer Tremblay fasten the free end of a pair of handcuffs to the foot of Mrs. Williams' antique, cast iron stove. The other end cuff was around my ankle. I stood there, astonished that he'd been able to crawl all the way from the opposite end of the kitchen, and by the time I understood what had just happened, he'd moved beyond my reach, finally slumping inertly against a row of cabinets.

He and the handcuff key are out of my reach. The stove is too heavy for me to lift or move. There are wisps of smoke drifting up from the basement and I can hear the flames licking at the steps.

I think I have a problem.

STAKEOUT

It was bitterly ironic that Carter failed to lock his car door that late afternoon when he finally caught up to Kaszlow. Like most of Kaszlow's lairs, this was a crumbling tract house in a low income project, windows shuttered, postage stamp lawn littered with fast food wrappers and other debris, paint cracked and flaking.

The front door was likely to be boobytrapped. Kaszlow was overconfident but not stupid. Carter walked around the house, found a window which seemed safe, mounted over the kitchen sink.

He returned to the rusting Pinto for his equipment and discovered his mistake. The zipper bag and its contents were missing.

There was no sign of the thief. Carter glanced at his watch. "Damn!" Less than an hour before darkness, certainly no time for a round trip to his motel room. He'd have to improvise.

With a rag wrapped around his hand, Carter smashed the kitchen window, cleared away the shattered glass and climbed into the house.

The rooms were all poorly furnished and filthy. Kaszlow selected for privacy, not the amenities. The basement door was in the hall, under the staircase. Carter tried the lightswitch and was pleasantly surprised to discover that it worked, although the small bulb did little more than disperse the shadows crowding around the foot of the staircase.

He descended carefully.

Kaszlow's coffin lay behind the water heater, under a small slit window covered with black felt. Carter approached cautiously. During the three years he'd been pursuing Kaszlow, he had found seven coffins, each untenanted.

The lid was well oiled and failed to creak melodramatically when he lifted it. Carter froze as he stared down into the motionless face of Nils Kaszlow, vampire.

He lowered the lid carefully, silently, even though Kaszlow would not wake before his time even if the house exploded. It was growing dark rapidly. Carter would have to move quickly.

Upstairs, he searched desperately for something he could fashion into the tool he needed. The couch and chairs were modern, plastic and fabric on an aluminum frame, unsuitable for his purposes. But the dining room table was a chintzy, imitation mahogany, the legs designed to be removed easily.

It wasn't as sharp as he would have liked, but one end was reasonably pointed and it would have to do. From the living room window, he could see the sun, an orange crescent, dipping toward the horizon.

This time he threw back the coffin lid with a flourish, so that it bounced against its stays and remained upright. It was going to be awkward without a sledgehammer, but the memory of his dead family was enough to overcome Carter's uncertainties. He raised his makeshift stake high into the air with both hands, and then slammed it down into Kaszlow's chest.

Carter was a strong man, empowered by years of anguish and hatred. The table leg stopped only when it reached the lower surface of the casket.

The deed done, his adrenaline rush rapidly dissipating, Carter staggered up out of the musty basement and threw himself onto the couch, exhausted physically and emotionally. Now that the long quest for revenge was complete, he felt a sudden uncertainty. With his family and job gone, his very sanity tottering, Carter was confused and frightened about the future.

His agitation hadn't diminished appreciably when Kaszlow walked into the room.

"My God!" Carter turned to face his nemesis, but lacked the strength to rise. "How can you be alive?" Or animate, anyway. Kaszlow hadn't been alive for at least a century.

The vampire's deeply lined face twisted into what might have been a smile. "You're wondering about this?" He was holding the table leg in his right hand, as though offering it to Carter.

"How could I have missed? It should have gone straight through your heart, you son of a bitch!" Could he have misjudged the angle, stupidly failed on the brink of success?

"Why, no, as a matter of fact." Kaszlow's English was quite good, but there was still the faintest trace of an accent. "A trifle off center perhaps, but remarkably accurate considering the crudity of your attack."

"Then how...?"

"Modern technology," Kaszlow answered pleasantly, moving to stand directly above Carter. "The small amount of actual wood pulp mixed into this synthetic paste won't even give me heartburn."

Carter was still laughing when the fangs bit into his throat.

THE SUBTERRINE, OR, 20,000 LEAGUES UNDER THE SOIL

The gopher class subterrine *Pellucidar*, owned and operated by Stryker Associates, crossed under the border separating Connecticut from New York less than ten hours following the outbreak of hostilities in the latest round of the Commerce Wars. Captain Lance Hewlitt was more than satisfied with the performance of the newly renovated warship, although only the more senior of the bridge crew correctly interpreted his stony silence and perpetual half frown.

"We appear to have entered enemy territory undetected, sir." Corporal Colby glanced up from his console. "I have a clear screen."

Hewlitt gave a just perceptible nod. "Have you found a target for us, Mr. Leonard?"

Lieutenant Scott Leonard turned away from his own terminal. "Three likelies, sir. The enemy will be attempting to resupply the stores in White Plains and Mamaroneck as quickly as possible, since they'll be the hardest to reach once we have more units in the area. Intelligence indicates major convoys are already en route, although they may well be using secondary roads as a precaution. Still, there are only a limited number of alternatives available to them."

The Captain nodded. "And the third?"

Leonard hesitated a moment, licked his lips before continuing. "A personal theory, sir. They'll be expecting pre-emptive strikes in both places and the convoys will be heavily escorted. On the other hand, if we bypassed the obvious targets and worked our way down the interstate toward New Rochelle, I think we might be able to find some prime targets near the new shopping mall that opened there last month."

The ensuing silence stretched while Hewlitt considered his options, finally nodded and turned to the warrant officer in charge of terrigation. "Mr. Wilson, proceed parallel to Interstate 95 for the time being. We will remain on amber alert while we are underway and within a half kilometer of the highway. Stay sharp, gentlemen. I don't need to remind you that this is not a training mission."

The *Pellucidar* shuddered slightly as CW2 Wilson entered a course correction. The ring of intake modules around its nose continued to operate smoothly, effectively dissolving the substance of everything that entered their fields of influence into constituent atoms, channeling them through the vacuum chamber that ringed most of the ship's hull, rebonding and expelling the mass through the out-takes sternward. Its passage through the earth was smooth and relatively silent, the displaced soil more homogeneous than it had been before, but otherwise unaffected. Or at least, almost so. The replaced mass was invariably somewhat more compact, occupying approximately one percent less volume than before conversion, and the effect was often perceptible on the surface, a rippling in the ground cover, the occasional more overt settling of buildings. The subterrine's wake could also be detected by sophisticated instruments mounted on telephone poles and bridge abutments alongside the highway, which was why the *Pellucidar*, and her sister ships like the *Lemuria* and the *Atlantis*, normally patrolled well away from the main roads, allowing sophisticated listening devices to advise them when a target was about to offer itself.

"Any signs of enemy activity?"

"No, sir," answered Colby, then hastily corrected himself. "Outside of the usual monitoring, I mean, sir. There are disturbance detectors operating at the limit of my screen, but their pattern indicates standard SI scanning."

"Traffic?"

"No anomalies."

Specialist Marie Rand turned in her chair and amplified. "Routine passenger traffic interspersed with heavier signatures probably indicating service vehicles."

"Probably?" This time Hewlitt's frown was genuine.

Rand paused for a double beat, but continued confidently. "Yes, sir. There are indications that the New York cartel has been accomplishing some resupply by transporting stock with lighter vehicles, vans, small panel trucks, and buses. On an individual basis it's impossible to distinguish the signature, but on an overall traffic level, it's clear that more cargo is being carried than normal. We're doing the same thing ourselves, particularly in the Danbury area."

Their progress was slow. Top speed even in the loosest soil was not much more than fifteen kilometers per hour. The *Pellucidar* followed a course roughly equidistant between I-95 and the Hutchinson River Parkway, bypassing the defensive facilities at Mamaroneck and Larchmont. In mid-afternoon, Hewlitt ordered a radical course change, descending to a depth of one thousand feet before crossing under Route 1. He had decided to bypass the New Rochelle defensive perimeter on the shoreward side and approach the mall area from the rear.

At 3:30, Specialist Rand broke a prolonged silence, her voice under control but vibrant with excitement. "Sir, I have multiple target readings coming from the southwest."

"Proximity?" There was a sudden crispness in Hewlitt's voice.

"ETA thirty minutes or less."

"Mr. Wilson?"

The warrant officer examined his terminal critically before answering. "There's an off ramp at heading eight zero, sir, and another at eight four. Either would be a viable exit if New Rochelle is their destination."

Hewlitt nodded to himself. "Or they could be continuing on toward Rye. How many targets?"

Rand shook her head. "Too many to count from this distance, sir. I'd make it twenty, perhaps thirty signatures."

"Mr. Wilson, how long would it take us to set up at the furthest of the two off ramps?"

"Eighteen minutes, sir, if we ascend as we go."

That would make targeting an iffy proposition, but Hewlitt was reluctant to chance setting up his ambush at the second exit and finding that his quarries had left the highway. There would not be sufficient time left to intercept them before they reached the mall and, although a subterrine attack on a mall had proven itself possible, the Mu had been destroyed demonstrating that it was not advisable.

"Go to red alert," Hewlitt ordered.

The *Pellucidar* reached a point fifty meters below the surface inside the "V" created by the highway and the off ramp. Rand released a mini-camera which tunneled up to the surface, then launched itself into the air, transmitting enhanced pictures to her console.

"Sir, I have a display."

"Bring it up on the main monitor, Ms Rand."

Immediately the large screen at one end of the bridge switched to a view of the surface, a long stretch of pavement marching toward the horizon. The near traffic was of little interest, but at the limit of vision, a cluster of heavier vehicles was already visible.

"Enhancement!" Hewlitt leaned forward in the command seat, squinting at the display. The picture swelled once, then again, and now he could see a long line of trucks, tractor trailers bearing the names Consolidated, Interstate, Trans-America, Continental, and others.

"No sign of escort, sir," reported Colby, "but I'm picking up a lot of engine signatures I can't rule out. Some of them pretty big."

"Could be tandems," commented Lieutenant Leonard. "They don't ordinarily use them in this area, but if they're hoping to build a quick stock surplus and wait us out, they might have waved normal procedure."

Hewlitt nodded, more to himself than the others. "We'll be cautious nevertheless. I want two salvoes, people. First strike will run from vehicles six to ten when six reaches the beginning of the off ramp. Salvo two will be against vehicles one throughfive. You'll have to calculate two vectors, one for the ramp, one for the highway, since we still don't know which way they'll go."

"Should I ready a third salvo, sir?" It was the first time the weaponry officer, Lieutenant Chu, had spoken. This was her first combat mission and tension crackled in her voice.

"As time permits, Lieutenant. If there's an escort, we won't have time to use it. If not, we should be able to pick off a few of the survivors in the confusion."

Tension built steadily during the next few seconds. The rectangular shapes of the distant trucks grew steadily in size as the lead vehicle, a shiny new ICF cab pulling an unmarked box, neared the exit. Although the air spargers were going full blast, everyone on the bridge was perspiring heavily as the truck slowed, then turned to its right, edging over toward the ramp.

"I have target acquisition, Captain." Rand's voice was professionally calm and level, but if anyone had turned in her direction, they would have noticed her taut pose, fingers poised to enter the firing sequence.

Hewlitt waited until the sixth truck was just turning away from the main road before speaking. "Fire!"

There was a just perceptible vibration as the five forward torpedo tubes discharged their contents, comparatively diminutive replicas of the *Pellucidar* itself, although in their case the matter converters were running full throttle, propelling the slim missiles at rates close to sixty kilometers per hour through the soil, operating at such intensity that their engines would overheat and self destruct in less than ninety seconds. But that was more than enough time for them to reach their targets.

As the torpedoes approached the trucks, they made slight course corrections. Internal guidance computers were linked to sophisticated sensors that searched for the effluvia of diesel fuel, allowing the homing program to differentiate between legitimate commercial targets and smaller, private vehicles. Their course curved gently upward until the dorsal surfaces broke the surface just an instant before impact.

There was the shudder of an explosion and then, so quickly that they could not be differentiated, four more. The display was lost as well, the first blast disturbing the delicate controls of the remote for a few seconds, although Rand quickly re-established control.

Six trucks were in flames, five struck by torpedoes, one damaged when its driver lost control and rammed into the wreckage. The *Pellucidar* was automatically taping the display so that damage assessment could be completed later; there was no time to gloat at the moment.

"Second salvo ready, sir!"

"Fire!" Another burst rippled through the soil. Hewlitt didn't wait to see them strike before turning to the navigator.

"Get us underway, Mr. Wilson. Bring us to heading six three."

The options available to the convoy were limited. Two trucks had already pulled over to the breakdown lane, but only so that they could bypass the burning wreckage and rush onward. Others were rolling to a stop even as the second salvo began to detonate.

"Four hits, sir. The last either missed or malfunctioned."

Hewlitt regretted the loss, but he still had ten confirmed kills and there was time to maneuver for at least one more full salvo. Judging by what had been visible on the display, they'd destroyed valuable cargo, consumer goods for the most part - electronic equipment, clothing, at least one container of plush furniture. With the shelves empty in their local stores, New Yorkers would stream across the border to buy in nearby Connecticut, where huge stockpiles had been assembled in anticipation of this conflict.

But as the *Pellucidar* passed under I-95, maneuvering for a second shot, Corporal Colby threw cold water on the bridge staff's enthusiasm. "Sir, I have an anomaly. One of the targets has changed signature."

"Can we get a visual?"

Colby called out coordinates and Rand ordered the remote to rise and adjust its angle of coverage. The surviving trucks were parting to either side of the highway, while a larger one painted a deep ebony roared up the centerline. "Sir, that's a mole!" Lieutenant Leonard commented unnecessarily.

"Secure firing stations. Mr. Wilson, take us out of here. Course at your discretion."

The warrant officer didn't bother to reply as the maneuvering lights came up. The deck tilted under their feet as the *Pellucidar* dropped her nose and began to burrow into the earth at a shallow angle. Depth would help, but it was more important to put some distance between themselves and the highway. Fortunately, the mole couldn't leave the pavement, although her hunter-seeker weaponry had a much more extensive range than the subterrine's own armament.

Rand maintained the link to the remote for as long as possible, and they were provided with an ominous close up view of their adversary. The mole was essentially a flat bed truck equipped with an oversized engine, its cargo area filled with weapons racks. The hunter-seekers they carried made use of the same burrowing technology as that of the subterrine, but they were designed to travel at reduced speeds and for much longer distances before their fuel was exhausted, searching for the distinctive vibrations of the matter converters. The last image the remote transmitted before it failed showed the weapons crews scrambling to winch two of the cylindrical devices into position.

Hewlitt watched the depth gauge and when he was satisfied they were deep enough, he ordered Chu to release chaff. Seconds later, a score of fist sized remotes were released from the stern, each equipped with a primitive converter, their tiny engines dispersing them in a pattern designed to intercept the hunter-seekers.

The tension was reduced rather than aggravated by the first concussive wave which struck the *Pellucidar* a minute later. One of the hunter-seekers had been fooled by the chaff and exploded harmlessly. A direct hit against a subterrine was unlikely under ordinary circumstances, but it was the concussive waves transmitted through the earth that were dangerous. The converters on the hull were sensitive and not easily repaired from the inside. It was theoretically possible to leave a submerged vessel and effect repairs from the exterior, but the amount of earth that would have to be displaced manually made this impractical. Even with its reserves of oxygen, the *Pellucidar* could not survive long without approaching the surface to freshen the tanks.

The second explosion was closer. The floor jumped under their feet and had it not been for their seat belts, several members of the bridge crew would have been thrown to the floor. Warning lights flashed but there were no audible alarms; any such sound would make it easier for the enemy to get a fix on their location.

"Damage?" Hewlitt asked quietly.

Chu checked with engineering before reporting. "We've lost some converters but not enough to overcome the redundancy factor. Ten percent loss in forward velocity though."

"Your assessment, Mr. Leonard?"

The lieutenant licked his lips. "We should be at the limit of their effective range in less than sixty seconds, sir. If they haven't already launched a follow up, we should be clear."

"Colby?"

"No tracking of any additional devices, sir. I'd say we could go to amber."

"What's your course, Mr. Wilson?"

The navigator read off coordinates. Hewlitt glanced at the map display on his own terminal, then ordered the *Pellucidar* to turn east, back toward the Connecticut border. "Level us off, Mr. Wilson."

Their first engagement had been a success.

During the next ten days, the *Pellucidar* ranged from New Rochelle to Scarsdale, as far east as Port Chester and north to the outskirts of Armonk, occasionally picking off isolated tractor trailers trying to slip through the blockade, twice encountering convoys, although they were never able to inflict as much damage as on their first outing. And in the second instance, disaster struck.

Five trucks had fallen prey to their initial salvo, but the planned followup was aborted when three moles bearing the Eagle Claw trademark of Blake Protection Services broke from the pack. Hewlitt ordered a crash dive and the usual evasive maneuvers, but the words were hardly out of his mouth when an explosion so close they could hear as well as feel it threw the bridge into turmoil.

There was no way the moles could have launched that quickly; they had to have struck a mine.

Both sides had discontinued laying mines following the tragic explosion of an Apex Corporation mine two years earlier when a passing tour bus with a poorly tuned engine fooled it into believing a subterrine was within its operational range. Theoretically, both sides had retrieved the devices they had planted following the Montgomery Ward Treaty, but the Apex Model Four had been equipped with a defective radio transmitter which often refused to respond to codes broadcast by friendly vessels, making recovery and even identification impossible. Consequently, many of them remained in place, patiently waiting for an excuse to self destruct.

"Damage?"

The reports were not reassuring. They had lost all their former velocity and suffered major converter damage. "We're dead in the dirt, Captain. Given a few hours to work on it, we could probably get up to half speed, but even that might be too optimistic a prediction. There's some hull damage and that's going to effect the alignment."

Hewlitt pursed his lips. "Rand, where are those moles?"

Rand had re-established contact with her remote, but the main display screen was out of commission and she was the only one who could see what was taking place on the surface above. "They're moving into attack position, sir. One of them's pretty far off, but the other two are straddling our position. We're still in the flat, sir. They can run right up on top of us."

"Weaponry. What have we got that's still operational?"

"Forward tubes are out, Captain." Chu had grown more confident during the course of their combat tour, but the worry was back in her voice now. "Stern tubes are questionable."

"All right. Rig for silent running. Shut down all non-essential systems."

"Should I release chaff, sir?"

"No, Lieutenant Chu. If we're stopped, the chaff won't move far enough away to do us any good, and it will just make a wider target sphere for our friends upstairs."

Seconds passed and Rand spoke again. "They're almost directly overhead, sir, and slowing down. I think they know we've stopped."

"The lead mole's one of their newer models," added Leonard. "They'll have picked up the explosion and probably know, or guess, that we've taken damage."

"The third one's coming up now, sir. They're stopping as well."

Hewlitt considered his options. They were few. The *Pellucidar* was immobilized and effectively defenseless. They could sit and wait to be killed, or they could radio to the surface and surrender. He didn't care for either option.

"They're positioning hunter-seekers, sir. I see four, no, six cradles swinging out."

Hewlitt was pleased to hear no tremor in her voice. This was a good crew, the best he'd ever commanded. As much as he hated the prospect of spending the rest of the war interned in some New York sub-assembly camp or sentenced to warehouse work under the rules of the Sears Convention, he owed it to these fine men and women to give them the opportunity to live and fight some other day.

He was about to order Colby to radio their surrender to the surface when Rand turned from her screen, and this time her voice was different. But it was confused rather than frightened.

"Sir, they're bringing the hunter-seekers back aboard and signaling for a parley."

Three hours later, a crippled *Pellucidar* was underway back toward the border, moving at half speed, but with its internal systems stable and minimally operational. The ever fluctuating corporate structure had, for once, worked to their benefit. At the very moment they struck the mine, their employers in the Connecticut Consortium had successfully concluded negotiations to purchase Blake Protection Services outright. The realignment order had reached the commander of the mole task force just as she was about to initiate her attack on the disabled subterrine.

Under the rules of commercial warfare, the moles were free to leave New York territory without hindrance but were prohibited from providing assistance to pre-aligned hostile forces, so Hewlitt and his crew had to make their own repairs.

At their reduced speed, it was dawn before they crossed into friendly territory, and almost noon when their bow broke the ground surface in the Greenwich Land Navy Yards. When Captain Hewlitt exited through the airlock, he found the Yardmaster sitting in a parked jeep waiting for him.

"Looks like you've taken some damage, Captain."

Hewlitt nodded. "We've lost a third of our converters and half that many again are juryrigged. Some structural damage as well, particularly in the starboard bow sections. Nothing you won't be able to handle, Yardmaster."

"Well, as to that, we have something of a problem."

Hewlitt raised an eyebrow.

The Yardmaster glanced at his watch. "What time did you return to friendly soil, Captain Hewlitt?"

"At a few minutes before six o'clock this morning." A sudden suspicion crystallized into certainty even as he spoke. "You don't mean..."

The Yardmaster shook his shaggy head. "Yes, I'm afraid I do. As of 5:00 AM local time, Stryker Associates became a wholly owned subsidiary of Sorada Interstate. Sorada is currently a division of the New York State Trading Cartel and, since you entered Connecticut after the transfer of ownership, the *Pellucidar* is in fact legally a hostile vessel. I'm afraid, Captain Hewlitt, that you and your crew are now prisoners of war."

Hewlitt sighed. The Yardmaster was alone and unarmed and there was nothing stopping him from re-entering the *Pellucidar* and ordering them underway. But it would be suicide. The defensive perimeter of the Greenwich Yards were as close to impregnable as made no difference, from either direction, and his crippled ship wouldn't stand a chance.

"It's not so bad, Captain," the Yardmaster continued, recognizing the other man's unspoken surrender. "You'll be interned in the Greenwich Shopping Center until a prisoner exchange is arranged." He paused, then winked. "And they're running a Resumed Trade Hostilities Sale all this month. If you shop around carefully, you ought to be able to make a real killing."

MILK CURDLING HORROR

The trouble all started because George Wentzler wanted to be a good vampire.

Actually, George didn't want to be a vampire at all, but he didn't have much choice after he'd unwisely taken a roundabout route back to his hotel during a vacation trip to New Orleans. Someone had called out to him from the shadows, a woman's voice. Although he'd intended to give her a wide berth and move on, assuming she was either a beggar or a thief, there'd been something about her eyes that held his attention and then his feet refused to move and...well, you can fill in the rest. It's not really relevant to this story.

Anyway, George was left to figure out things on his own. His first clue was the annoying sunburn that plagued him for the next few days, even though it was mid-November. Then the insomnia, loss of appetite, and a sudden violent allery to garlic. By Thanksgiving, he already knew what had happened, at least on some subliminal level, but it wasn't until he found himself unable to even taste his mother's painstakingly prepared turkey dinner that he finally was forced to face the truth.

Pleading illness, George rushed home, thawed out a frozen steak, and sucked out the juices. The blood didn't exactly restore him, but it confirmed his suspicions. George had become a vampire.

Fortunately, he already worked the nightshift, so that part of the adjustment was fairly simple. To his pleasant surprise, religious symbols did not cause him to shrink away in terror and he actually prayed for guidance in a local church, ceasing only when he realized he was staring with naked desire at the neck of another parishioner.

He couldn't possibly attack another human being. For one thing, vampirism did not after all bring with it the superhuman strength displayed in various movies. George was small of build, if not actually frail. Nor could he have lived with himself if he'd been responsible for killing or converting anyone else.

So George chose the only alternative available to him. Every third or fourth night, when the hunger became irresistible, he drove to work by way of various back roads, threading his way through a series of dairy farms. Sooner or later he'd spot one of the cows grazing in a field or nodding sleepily near a fence. George would pull over, wait a few minutes to make certain he was unobserved, then move quickly through the darkness. Even then he drank with as much moderation as possible, never killing his victim, just drawing enough of the life source to cool his own internal fires.

After several months, George actually attained a level of peace with himself and his altered nature, feeling that his life was once more in balance.

But already the consequences were beginning to manifest themselves.

The first recorded incident was hardly noteworthy. Oscar Heffernan, a small scale dairy farmer, showed up one morning at the local emergency room. His left hand was deeply lacerated, requiring extensive stitching.

"The goddamned cow up and bit me," he complained. "Never seen nothing like it before. Wasn't as though I hurt 'er or anything. Didn't even have the goddamned milking machine attached to 'er yet."

Next came the affair of the mangled sheep. Richard Olin was not a dairy farmer. His grandfather had given up on livestock before Richard was born and planted neat rows of apple trees in what had once been pastureland. But Richard's son was a 4-H Club enthusiast and his father had supported the boy's plan to raise a few sheep.

All four animals, two adults and two lambs, were found dead one morning in early March. Their throats had been torn out and their bodies bitten and chewed, although there was no evidence that any of the meat had actually been eaten. The surprisingly small amount of blood at the scene caused the authorities to hint darkly of satanist cults and strange rituals.

Both incidents were repeated with variations over the course of the next few weeks. Another farmer shot one of his prize breeding stock after the animal bit off his ear. Hunters reported surprisingly little game in the area, but often stumbled across mangled but uneaten remains. Some theorized a seriously ill bobcat was at large, taking out its internal pain on every living thing it encountered.

Then someone realized that the total output from the local dairy industry was down dramatically. Farmers complained that their stock was alternately listless (during the day), and unnaturally restless (during the night). There were rumors of some new strain of bovine encephalitis, and scientists from the university took blood samples and captured mosquitoes. Although many of the cows they tested were anemic, there were no detectible foreign bodies in their blood.

Arthur Caldwell was the first to hold the key to the mystery, although he didn't realize it at the time. One Sunday morning, he rousted Sheriff Parsons out of bed at the crack of dawn, complaining that local pranksters had gotten hold of one of his best milkers.

"They must've doped her, then dragged her out of the pasture and winched her up into that there tree." Sure enough, Honeybee had greeted the morning draped over the lower branches of a large oak.

"It's almost as if Honeybee grew a set of wings during the night and flew into that tree," commented Sheriff Parsons.

Although it would be several weeks yet before there was any official recognition of the true state of affairs, some of the local people already suspected. Strands of garlic were seen in increasing numbers, twisted around strands of barbed wire, tied to barn doors, nailed to the ends of watering troughs.   Father Gilhallen of the local Catholic Church was petitioned to bless the local herds. Perhaps fearing that he'd look foolish, the priest dissembled for several days before finally giving in to community pressure. Unfortunately, he was mauled by Sid Doyle's Angus bull at his very first stop. It could be said that Father Gilhallen was at least partly a victim of his own pomposity; to avoid being photographed in what he considered an undignified activity, he'd arrived at the Doyle farm before sun-up.

Aphrodite's Pizzeria was the next to suffer. Arnold Parsigian, the proprietor, was overwhelmed with complaints about a sour taste in his pizzas. Parsigian insisted that he had not changed his recipe in twenty years, that if anything was different, it must be something wrong with the raw materials he received from his suppliers. After several complaints, the Board of Health sent in investigators, who ascertained that everything Parsigian used was up to standard. The pepperoni was fresh and unadulterated, the tomato sauce, yeast, cheese and other ingredients were kept refrigerated until they were ready to be used, and they could find nothing to fault in the way the pizzas were prepared.

Nevertheless, Parsigian's cheese immediately soured when it came into contact with his garlic enhanced tomato sauce, a situation which did not end until he finally switched to a non-local dairy supplier.

The first eyewitness account was dismissed at the time because of the unreliability of its source. Billy Winters and Dolph Watson had gone for a joyride in Billy's father's brand new convertible, taking along a couple of six packs for entertainment. The extensive damage the vehicle suffered that evening was assumed to be the result of their having driven off the road somewhere. Obviously the story they'd energetically told to everyone who'd listen was too outlandish to be credible.

"I'm tellin' ya, these cows sort of swooped down on us, like." Billy did most of the talking, while Dolph just nodded his head and inserted the phrase "he's tellin' it like it is" whenever his friend stopped for breath.

"They landed all around us, see, and one of them, the biggest of 'em, I think, it landed right on the hood, see? Those dents there are where its hooves pushed it in. Anyway, it looked in through the windshield at us and it opened its mouth and there were these big fangs."

No one in town, least of all Billy's outraged and unforgiving father, was about to accept the existence of a pack of vampire cows.

But before long, the truth became inescapable. Arthur Caldwell consulted a veterinarian when his stock flatly refused the fodder he'd thrown down for them. "They looked at me like they was saying, 'we don't eat...grass', or something." Residents in the area reported seeing large objects hurtling through the night sky, and some reported a bizarre sound. "It was kind of like an evil, drawn out moooooooo!, you know?" offered Dale Hammerfield.

The climax was precipitated by young Jennie Danielson, only six years old, whose childish curiosity almost caused a tragedy. Her parents were watching a mindless sitcom on television when she heard something bumping at the rear door. Since Jennie was a curious child and it was clear that her parents weren't going to budge, she walked out into the kitchen and turned on the outside light.

There was a large Jersey cow standing on the back patio.

Mindful of her parents' admonition never to leave the house alone after dark, Jennie wouldn't step outside, but she really wanted to reach out and pet that cow. There was something about its eyes, so deep and magical, that made her want to ignore everything she'd been taught. But the conditioning was too strong. She opened the door and moved to the threshold, but would not go one step further.

"Why don't you come on inside if you want to be petted," she said softly, knowing her parents would not approve. But they hadn't expressly forbidden her to invite large animals inside either.

And with that, the cow smiled malevolently and surged forward.

Tom and Betty Danielson were roused by their daughter's screams, arrived in the kitchen to find her hiding under the table while a black and white spotted monster with dripping fangs and a ceasely whisking tail tried to drag her out. Tom raced upstairs for his shotgun, while Betty picked up a broom and began berating the beast with the handle. Aroused, it reared up and knocked her away with one casual sweep of a forehoof. The broomhandle caught between Betty's ribcage and the kitchen wall and snapped jaggedly into two pieces.

Groggy, but determined to save her daughter, Betty struck again, this time with the sharp point of the shattered broom. The wooden shaft fortuitously entered the creature's body just behind the foreshoulder and pierced the upper right corner of the beast's heart.

With one terrible, final scream, it leaped straight into the air and collapsed into a corner of the kitchen. Within seconds, its body had dissolved into a mass of putrescence that smelled distinctly like very sour milk.

The rest is a matter of public record. The initial skepticism of the authorities did not restrain the populace at large, which organized itself into several vigilante groups. Despite the protests of the farmers involved, every dairy cow within the county was similarly skewered before night fell the following day. Approximately a third of them deliquesced spectacularly as they died.

As for George Wentzel, who unwittingly started all of this, he belatedly realized that he was responsible. He still gets his blood supply from farm animals, but now he draws it out artificially first, to avoid the danger of infection.

Even vampires subscribe to some standards of decorum.

THE LAST DEMON

On his 666th birthday, Ogerak the Offputting escaped from Hell into the world of humans. It wasn't really his birthday since demons aren't actually born, but transmogrificationday is a far less satisfying term. When he noticed that the Portal had been momentarily left unguarded while an influx of newly lost souls was arriving to begin their eternal penance, he acted on impulse, hunching his shoulders so as not to be noticed among the throng as he made his way back against the tide of damned humanity and so crossed over, determined to find his destiny, or at least enjoy a break from his tedious existence.

It is not easy being the very last of the one hundred thousand demons to be created. For one thing all of the really nifty names were gone, along with most of the formidable body enhancements. Ogerak didn't even have claws, his tail was vestigial, and his horns were invisible under his unruly hair. He was tall and broad shouldered and spectacularly ugly but even without a magical enchantment, he could quite easily pass for human.

Ogerak hesitated when he stepped out of the Portal, wondering if this had perhaps been a mistake. He had never been to the human world before and the stories he had heard over the centuries from more senior demons – and all of them were more senior – were contradictory and no doubt distorted by memory, or more likely caprice. Demons lived only to inflict torment and confusion, even upon one another. But if Ogerak was having second thoughts, it was too late to act upon them. The Portal closed behind him and he hadn't the slightest idea how to open a new one.

It was very dark, but Ogerak was used to the absence of light. He was standing in an empty lot flanked by tall buildings in every direction. He could hear faint traffic noises in the distance which he mistakenly interpreted as the muted roars of predators. Since his immediate surroundings appeared to be deserted, he set off toward a cluster of lights he could barely discern in the distance.

Moments later he encountered his first humans, or to be more precise, his first living humans. He was traversing a narrow, cluttered passage between two buildings when three figures separated themselves from the shadows and barred his way just as he stepped into a pool of light cast from a fixture above one of the doors. Ogerak stopped and blinked, wondering what this portended. "I am Ogerak," he announced. "Tremble in the presence of my puissant evilness." All of the really good personal catch phrases had also been taken by the other demons.

There was a muted sound that might have been suppressed laughter but which Ogerak chose to interpret as panicky obeisance. One of the figures stepped into the light. "Hey, Dude, this is Troll territory and you have to pay to use our alley. It's sort of a troll road, get it?"

Ogerak blinked and examined the figure more closely. "I have worked with trolls, I know trolls, some of my friends are trolls. Imposter, you are no troll."

He took a menacing step forward into the light and the one who had spoken took a balancing step backward. "Hey, you're a big fellow, aren't you? I like the tattoos on your cheeks. They're classy. And the leather outfit isn't bad either."

Ogerak blinked in confusion. "Tattoos? Are you referring to the Cicatrices of Coryphon, inscribed on my face to honor my service to the Nether Realms?"

"Nether Realms? Who are they? I know every gang in the city and I never heard of them. Hey, you must be from out of town."

Ogerak nodded. "I am a visitor here as you surmise. Could you perhaps direct me to the master of the city so that I might pay my respects?"

"Well, just at the moment, you might say that I was master of the city, at least as far as you're concerned. And you'll pay alright, but not just your respects."

Ogerak frowned and his face became even more offputting. "I detect insolence in your tone. Do you venture to challenge me?"

The human moved his arm and there was the flash of light on metal. "If you're looking for a fair fight, Dude, then you've come to the wrong place. Now let's see some money or I'm gonna have to cut you."

Ogerak had never been in this situation before. As juniormost demon, it was he who issued challenges, all of which had to date failed. But he knew the proper response. The human's soul was hopelessly lost so he lunged forward with surprising quickness for one with such a large body, his jaws already dislocating to accommodate their distension, and he bit off the human's head before the latter had time to react. The body remained erect for a second, then fell quietly to the ground. Ogerak swallowed the head – it was rather too salty for his taste and he wasn't really hungry – and looked around for the other two humans, who were running at full speed toward the far end of the alley rather than proffering their obeisance. He considered this a shocking lapse of manners.

For the next few minutes, he waited for the body to produce a new head so that he could interrogate the former master of the city about the attributes of his domain, but nothing happened. This puzzled and upset Ogerak. The losers in a challenge always regenerated promptly back in Hell, at which point they graciously acknowledged their defeat. Perhaps the process took longer in the human world. Impatient, he decided to dispense with a formal capitulation and set off once more, this time confident with the knowledge that he, Ogerak, was now master of the city.

Moments later three demons materialized at the exact spot where Ogerak has earlier stepped out of the Portal. For a split second, a theoretical observer might have noticed claws and fangs and prehensile tails, but then the masking charm took effect and the threesome appeared only as vaguely disreputable humans with no fashion sense.

The threesome had been sent to reclaim Ogerak. Murmural the Maleficent was the team leader, with Nuramor the Noxious and Inkarion the Irritating as backup. Murmural had been to the human world before, though not since the 14th Century, while his companions were on their first visit. Murmural expected that it would be a very brief excursion. A demon as inexperienced as Ogerak must have drawn attention to himself almost immediately upon arriving. Onorus the Overbearing – currently in charge of the Office for Suppression of Forbidden Awareness - would be very unhappy if Ogerak had revealed his true nature to any humans. The demonic truant would be in very big trouble if that was the case.

"Follow," Murrmural commanded and set off, trying unsuccessfully to detect Ogerak's scent.

Ogerak had proceeded only a few more blocks before the hair on his back bristled under his leather vest. Trusting his demonic instincts, he paused and carefully examined his surroundings. On the opposite side of the street, a dim light showed inside an otherwise darkened building. In the window facing him he perceived a fearsome array of beasts.

Undaunted – he was after all master of the city – Ogerak crossed to confront the danger directly. "I am Ogerak. Tremble in the presence of my puissant evilness." Most of the creatures remained quiescent but one rose onto its hindquarters and pressed its nose against the glass, wagging a not at all vestigial tail furiously back and forth. Ogerak was momentarily nonplused, not having expecting such a direct challenge, but he was prepared to defend his prerogatives against all comers.

Something growled softly behind him and Ogerak spun – or turned at least – to see a much larger creature approaching. Indeed the newcomer was considerably bigger than was Ogerak himself. It had two large glowing eyes and a crest that cycled between red and blue in a hypnotic rhythm as it advanced. Ogerak was perplexed by its manner of locomotion since there are no wheels in Hell. Wheels might make some tasks easier for the damned, after all.

The creature addressed him in a booming voice. "YOU THERE! STEP AWAY FROM THE BUILDING AND LET ME SEE YOUR HANDS!"

The tone was so peremptory that Ogerak obeyed without thinking. The voice very much resembled that of Astoriak the Appalling, his immediate supervisor back in Hell. If he had responded to the instructions in the correct order, all might have been well, but he extended his arms before stepping clear and one of them crashed through the window. The diminutive monsters began emitting a variety of upsetting noises and two of them jumped down onto the sidewalk. One had the temerity to sniff his ankle.

ALL RIGHT, STOP WHERE YOU ARE! RAISE YOUR HANDS AND PLACE THEM ON THE WALL!" The larger creature began to wail and it moved suddenly forward. Ogerak found himself beset by danger from front and rear and he panicked, although he later characterized his action as swift and prudent withdrawal.

Although he was a bit overweight and definitely out of condition, he managed a quite acceptable sprint to the nearest corner and turned to his right, eyes darting about in search of sanctuary. The wailing increased in pitch and volume and Ogerak slipped into the first alleyway he encountered, confident that his pursuer was too large to follow. Three blocks later he crouched concealed in a dumpster as the wailing creature, which was silent now, moved slowly past.

Ogerak was extremely uncomfortable. The temperature had dropped into the upper eighties and he shivered with the cold. It began to rain and he hated getting wet. And as the minutes slid past, he began to feel hungry. When the rain finally died away shortly before dawn, he slipped out of his hiding place and set off in search of food. He tried some of the debris from the dumpster and was surprised to find it completely inedible. Although he usually fed on the damned – the supply was inexhaustible since they always regenerated – Ogerak often dined otherwise for the sake of variety. In Hell, even rocks were magically transformed when ingested by a demon but here, he realized, they remained just rocks. So he set off to find real food. Something fresh.

The buildings remained dark but once he reached a better lit street, he saw a single human standing next to some enigmatic contrivance at an intersection. He approached cautiously, having decided to keep a low profile until he understood the rules of this world.

The human spun around as he drew near. "Hey there, big fellow. Shouldn't sneak up on a guy like that."

"I am Ogerak. Tremble in the presence of my puissant evilness." He paused for effect. "And tell me where I might find sustenance."

The human seemed to relax. "What are you? A street artist or just a homeless crazy?"

Ogerak had no idea what those terms referred to so he ignored the question. "I hunger. Can you help me in my quest?"

The human turned back to the artifact he'd been tending. "I'm not set up yet but I can manage a cold bagel and some cream cheese. It'll cost you though. Got any money?"

"What is this money of which you speak?"

"Cash. Moolah. Dinero. Bucks. Greenbacks. Coin of the realm. And I don't take plastic."

Ogerak shook his head. Demons were supposed to be able to understand and speak any conceivable human language but once again he had no idea what the human was talking about. "I have no knowledge of these things about which you speak."

"Foreigner, eh? Probably illegal. You got papers? A green card?"

Ogerak spread his hands eloquently. "I have nothing but what you see."

The human shook his head and turned away, then drew something out of bag and extended it toward Ogerak. "Here, take this. The raisin ones never sell anyway. But you'd better find yourself a job, under the table obviously, if you want to stay around here."

He sniffed the proffered item. "What manner of flesh is this?"

"It's not meat, loonie. It's a bagel. Baked in ovens."

Ogerak smiled, which actually made him look more fearsome. "My first duty was tending the ovens. But I desire more hearty fare. I am, after all, master of the city."

The human sighed. "Yeah, you and the mayor are good buddies, I imagine. Look, this city chews up innocents like you and spits them out. You'd better wise up or hit the road."

Ogerak pondered what profit might be derived from striking the pavement as he sniffed the bagel. He had been considering devouring the human, but the latter's sudden act of charity meant that he was not irretrievably damned after all and was therefore beyond Ogerak's power.

Those last few words had also given him pause. Obviously there was not the clear hierarchy in the human world that existed in Hell. Was this mayor superior to the master of the city or just a co-equal? And was the city itself an entity that could swallow him and expel him at any moment? He did not relish being chewed up. Regeneration always gave him a headache.

He swallowed the bagel, which was refreshingly stale, but it failed to appease the grumbling in his belly. With a last regretful look, he turned and stalked off, while the human muttered under his breath and turned back to his wares.

Ogerak wandered the city throughout the morning, gathering a few odd looks but far fewer than he might have expected. He saw little that was familiar, but he did manage to make friends with a colony of rats – there are rats in hell – and he eavesdropped on humans in order to learn what this money thing was and where he might find some. At first he stopped people at random and asked, but they either ran from him with a scream, which was a moderately comforting reminder of home, or shouted imprecations. One or two even threatened to assault him and it was only his growing sense of discretion that prevented Ogerak from dispatching them on the spot. All but one had been fair game.

Money, he learned, consisted of small pieces of green parchment which could be exchanged for goods. There were mystical symbols inscribed on them – a key, a pyramid, an all seeing eye – but he was unable to determine the nature of the magical spells they denoted. Ogerak was also at a loss to discover from whence came this script until he happened to notice a man emerging from a building with a handful of the parchment and inquired as politely as he could manage about where he had acquired it.

"The lobby's right through that doorway, asshole." Ogerak's most polite demeanor wasn't very. "Use your eyes. They're big enough."

Inside the building, Ogerak quickly ascertained the procedure. Humans stood in line until they reached one of several hooded windows, at which point another human dispensed the parchment from hiding. He considered bypassing the line since he was master of the city but decided to observe the process in more detail first.

And then he was at the head of the line. "Can I help you, sir?"

"I would like some money please."

"Do you have an account with us, sir?" The voice was bored. Ogerak recognized boredom; he had experienced it for 665 of his 666 years.

"I am newly arrived in this city and do not understand all of its customs, but I have need of money."

"Do you have a traveler's check then? Or something else to be cashed? A money order, perhaps?"

Ogerak was hungry and frustrated. "I have told you. I need money. I am Ogerak. Tremble in the presence of my puissant evilness and give me what I wish or take the consequences!"

The attendant recoiled and a moment later Ogerak heard something very much like the wailing sound of the monster that had chased him the night before. Desperate, he caught hold of the enclosure with both hands and tore it free, which generated a chorus of screams and much running about. He saw a tray filled with rows of the magical green parchment and snatched up two handsful, then turned and made his way hastily outside. The wailing must mean either that there was a similar monster dwelling within the building or that one was being summoned. He heard a popping sound behind him and a series of light jabs tickled him between the shoulderblades as he turned and began to run. Well, lumber. Running really wasn't one of his accomplishments.

The pursuit was more persistent this time and more than an hour passed before the wailing sounds subsided and Ogerak, who had broken into an abandoned warehouse, sat on the floor and tried various conjurations without finding one which would trigger whatever magical potential the green parchment contained. He finally gathered it up and tucked it neatly into a pocket in his harness.

Two blocks away, three figures had turned their heads toward the clamor. "Let us investigate," said Murmural. "The irritating Ogerak may have drawn attention to himself."

Inkarion protested. "It is I who irritate. The faithless Ogerak is merely offputting."

"Whatever," Murmural answered, rolling his eyes.

Purchasing food from street vendors proved to be relatively easy and the yawning chaos in Ogerak's gut was finally assuaged, at least for the time being, although a human would have been much more satisfying. He had managed to find a few who counted beast flesh among their wares, although for some reason they insisted upon burning it before they would allow consumption. As darkness began to fall, Ogerak decided to emulate the humans and rest indoors. He had even learned that some of the buildings in the city catered to travelers and that these were called hotels. He found one such that was suitably dirty and unkempt and asked the attendant to explain the procedure for acquiring temporary dwelling privileges.

"You pay the nightly fee, in advance. No drugs, no women, no loud noises." The attendant considered Ogerak's oversized frame. "Break anything and you pay for it."

Ogerak laid out all of his money on the counter. "Is this sufficient?"

The clerk's eyes opened widely and he nodded. "For one night, sure. But you'll need more if you're planning to stay any longer."

The money had already disappeared, confirming Ogerak's suspicion that it was magic.

"The depository is not likely to give me any more," Ogerak observed glumly.

"Depository? Oh, you mean the bank. Broke, huh? Don't you have a job, friend?"

Ogerak shrugged. "I have only what you see."

"Homeless too." The attendant shook his head. "Well, you'll have to get a job if you want more money, and you'll need more money if you want to stay here another night."

So that was it, thought Ogerak. The reason the attendant had been unwilling to give him money when he asked was because he had no job. He had not noticed that the humans were carrying such a thing, but perhaps they only produced it when they reached the window. "Where would I get one of these jobs?" he asked earnestly.

"They're pretty hard to come by. I feel for you, friend." This was patently false. "I was on the street for a while myself. If the guy who worked this desk before me hadn't up and died, I'd probably be there still."

Ogerak's brow wrinkled. "So you perform your duties here and your masters reward you with this job thing?"

"Well, sort of. Yeah."

"And once you have a job, the depository will dispense money at your request?"

"Within reason, yeah, depending on how much you get paid."

"And you succeeded to this post because of the death of your predecessor?"

"That's right."

"I understand." Ogerak smiled because he had already detected the distinctive odor of damnation, then unhinged his jaw and lunged forward.

It took the three demons several weeks to track Ogerak down and they ultimately found him by accident. They had entered the rundown hotel seeking lodging for the night and none of them had recognized the oversized desk clerk at first. He was wearing a shabby overcoat and his eyes were downcast and full of misery. Luckily Nuramor was hungry enough that he was examining humans closely hoping to find one of the irretrievably damned.

"Ogerak! Is that you?"

It was a moderately joyful reunion with much slapping of backs, punching of ribs, gnashing of teeth, and pulling of hair. Eventually Murmural called them to order and informed Ogerak that he was to be taken back to Hell, by force if necessary.

"On the contrary, I cannot wait to return. This world is a madhouse whose illogical rules have created an existence so unbearable that I now fully understand why humans sacrifice their immortal souls in order to escape. Here one must have a job, which is not simply assigned by a higher authority but which must be discovered by the individual, and only then if that individual possesses certain documents attesting to his personal history. But this history must be established by those same documents, a circular logic which makes them unobtainable save through subterfuge." Ogerak reached into the pocket of his overcoat and withdrew a battered wallet, opened it to display a social security card and driver's license. "I was forced to assume the identity of my former employer after I had eaten him."

Even Murmural found this hard to credit. The bureaucracy in the 14th Century had not been nearly so advanced.

"Nor can one survive with a single job. I myself spend my evenings ejecting boisterous individuals from warrens where rhythmic sounds are played at such a high volume that they inflict permanent damage on the hearing of those humans present. And don't get me started about their politics." He would have regaled them further with details of the horrific world in which he'd trapped himself, but Murmural intervened.

"It is time for you to return and face the consequences of your malingering. "

Ogerak beamed at him. "I welcome the ritual dismemberment. Let us be off."

Murmural glanced around. "Not here. I can only perform the ritual a single time and there must be ample space for the vortex to generate a Portal."

"There's a park at the end of the block. Would that be big enough?" Now that Ogerak had the chance to escape the human world, he was impatient to be gone.

"We shall see."

Presently, the four demons stood at the edge of the small fenced area. Two men with rakes stood on the far side but there was almost no other pedestrian traffic. "This should be adequate," decided Murmural. "It will only take a few moments to invoke the Portal. Let us proceed."

Murmural had barely uttered the first few syllables when they were interrupted. The two humans they'd noticed earlier were approaching, brandishing their rakes. "Hey! Can't you jokers read? Keep off the grass. We just finished seeding here."

Nuramor was so furious that his disguise began to slip but Murmural stepped in front of him until he had restored control. "Our apologies, gentlemen. We did not mean to transgress."

"Yeah, well, move along then. And try not to make too much of a mess on your way out."

They left while the two men efficiently raked over their tracks.

"This way," urged Ogerak. "There is a larger park only a few blocks away."

There were humans there as well, but it was indeed much larger and the demons were able to find an open space among a cluster of trees where they believed they would not be observed. Murmural began the invocation again and this time the opening stages went smoothly. Ogerak was exhilarated by the sight of a Portal beginning to form in the center of the clearing, spinning lights and gouts of flame slowly taking on substance.

The Portal was half formed when they were interrupted.

"Hey, buddy! You got a permit?"

Ogerak turned to see a uniformed man approaching rapidly. He moved to intercept. "Is there a problem, officer?"

"Not if you got a permit, there isn't. But if you don't, there's a very big problem." He glanced up at the coalescing Portal. "Pretty impressive, I'll give you that. But you need a permit to do any kind of performance art here. Particularly with pyrotechnics."

Ogerak sniffed but the policeman, though nearly a lost cause, was not beyond redemption and was therefore untouchable. He thought quickly. "You don't understand. This isn't a performance. My friend here is very religious and this is a miraculous event. Surely we don't need permits for miracles?"

"Well then, it seems we do have a problem after all. Use of public land for religious ceremonies is a violation of city ordinances.

I'm afraid your friend will have to cease and desist at once or I'll be forced to arrest him."

Ogerak began to protest, but the policeman stepped past before he could react and placed a hand on Murmural's shoulder. The senior demon started, shook his head, and the Portal began to oscillate. "Unhand me, human offal!" he shouted, forgetting himself, but it was too late. The outer rim of the half formed Portal began to break up and the center began to deliquesce.

They were dismissed with a stern warning that they hardly heard. On their way out of the park, Ogerak asked if Murmural could try again, perhaps at night.

"I lack the power to repeat the ritual. We'll have to wait for the next scheduled Portal." He grimaced. "Which won't be for twenty years. But it is merely a drop in the bucket compared to eternal damnation, after all."

Ogerak helped them settle in. Inkarion and Nuramor became tag team wrestlers for the WWL. Murmural hosted a radio talk show. Ogerak himself went back to managing the sleazy hotel. The years passed as a steady stream of minor torments and when the time finally approached when they would be able to return to Hell, Ogerak felt that he had survived the worst that the human world could possibly throw at him.

He was wrong, of course. Two weeks before the Portal was due, he was randomly chosen for audit by the IRS.

CORRUPTION IN OFFICE

When Paul Norton received the emergency summons to the Oval Office, he acknowledged the call curtly, then buzzed his chief assistant. "Anything hot, Bob?"

"No, sir. Nothing out of the ordinary. The coup in England seems to be winding down and there haven't been any ceasefire violations in Canada for almost a week."

"All right, thanks. I'm going over to the White House for a meeting. Hold the fort, will you?" He clicked off, tapped his finger impatiently for a few seconds, then asked his secretary to arrange transportation.

With her usual efficiency, she arranged for a private shuttle, which was ready and waiting by the time he had taken the elevator to the roof of the State Department office building.

A few minutes later, the pilot set him down on a small landing field on the White House grounds where armed guards remained attentive even after he passed through the scanners, grudgingly allowing him into the building.

Jennifer Frakes was waiting just inside. The jowly Chief of Staff had served President Torgeson for over twenty years, rising through the backrooms of the insurgent Unionist Party while Torgeson progressed from state representative to governor to senator to President.

"Morning, Jennifer. What's up" Norton glanced at his watch, frowned. "I thought the President was meeting with the King of Romania this morning."

"We've had some problems. His schedule has been suspended...indefinitely." It was voice rather than words that tipped him off that something was seriously wrong. Ordinarily, Frakes was gruff and overbearing, using force of will to maintain discipline among subordinates and associates alike. Uncertainty and hesitation were not among her attributes. "Come on. We'll talk in my office."

Once the door was closed, Frakes pointed to a chair and Norton sat. Frakes remained standing as she delivered the news. "The President is dead. He came down to his office early this morning, just as he always does, and apparently died almost immediately after arriving. One of his bodyguards found him a short time later, slumped over his desk, but it was too late for medical treatment, and he wisely called me instead of raising an alarm."

It took a few seconds for the meaning of the words to penetrate. Norton had never considered Torgeson a friend, but the man had been instrumental in his own spectacular rise from the parishes of New Orleans to head the State Department.

"I'm terribly sorry to hear that." The words came out automatically, but Norton realized they were sincere as well. Vice President Curtis was a frenetic, shallow man who had bluffed his way through several crises by disguising utter panic as ceaseless energy, and the prospect of him sitting in the Oval Office, even for the few months that remained before the election, was not pleasant.

"Does the Vice-President know?"

"No, and he's not going to."

Norton blinked. "I...uh...I don't understand."

Frakes leaned back, arms crossed, and stared directly into Norton's eyes. "Do you really think Samuel Curtis is capable of leading this country?"

"Well, no, as a matter of fact." His first inclination had been to dissemble, but perhaps because the shock of the revelation was beginning to sink in, he felt unable to remain evasive. "I think he'd be an utter disaster even in the best of times. With the budgetary crisis and the tax payers' revolt and the Republicrats gaining steadily in the polls, I think it would be a national as well as party disaster."

"Exactly. Curtis was only put on the ticket to keep the western states from leaving the Unionist Party. As Vice President, he's not in a position to do any real harm. We expected him to remain there through this year and Torgeson's second term."

"Which is now impossible." Norton's head was whirling. Who would the Unionist Party turn to now? The New Hampshire primary was only weeks away.

Frakes picked up a thick file from her desk, opened it as though to check something, then snapped it closed. "We did an extensive background check before Torgeson nominated you to be Secretary of State, you know."

"Of course."

"I understand that for several years, you served as a houngan in Lepatria Parish."

Norton felt as though the temperature in the room had just plummeted thirty degrees. "That was a baseless charge raised by my opponent when I was running for the state legislature."

Frakes made an impatient gesture. "Drop it, Norton. This is the big time here. We knew all about it before we approached you to join the cabinet. You covered your tracks extremely well, almost enough to throw us off. But the White House has people who specialize in finding the invisible. As a matter of fact, the efficiency with which you concealed your involvement in voodoo was one of the reasons we decided to put you in State. Deviousness is a prerequisite for that job, as I'm sure you've come to realize."

Although he thought about bluffing, Norton recognized a lost cause when he saw one. "All right, yes, I was involved in a very minimal way during my twenties. But I dropped it all ten years before I first ran for office."

"But you <u>were</u> a houngan."

"A very inept one." He laughed briefly, without humor. "That's one of the reasons I gave it up, to be honest. I seemed to have the talent, but not the control. Some of my magic...misfired."

"Have you ever raised a zombie?"

Norton started to shake his head, then realized the implications of the question. "You're not suggesting...?" Frakes' steady gaze never wavered. "You're serious, aren't you?"

"Absolutely. President Torgeson must serve out his term; no other solution is acceptable. If Curtis succeeds to the Presidency, he'll have at least months to ruin the party - if not the country - and it would be difficult to deny him the nomination to run for a term of his own."

"Even if Torgeson...serves out his term, there's no one of comparable stature for the campaign. The problem is delayed but not solved."

"True. But at least we buy some time."

"We could never bring it off. I mean, zombies aren't quite as graceless as they appear in the movies, but they lack any real spirit, their body temperature drops off, and they begin to smell after a while. Even their voices lack inflection." Not that Torgeson had ever been a particularly vibrant speaker, he thought silently.

Frakes made a dismissive gesture. "Mechanical details. We can work around them. After the last two assassination attempts, it won't surprise anyone if Torgeson cuts back on public appearances. We can use one of his doubles for the rare occasion when it's necessary, and televised speeches can be synthesized by computers accurately enough to escape detection."

It was hard for Norton to accept that Frakes was serious, but she was not known for her sense of humor. He began to wonder if this was some bizarre loyalty test she and Torgeson had dreamed up between them, to find out how he would react under stress.

As if she were reading his mind, Frakes stepped forward. "Come on."

"Where are we going?"

"I want you to take a look at the President. We have him laid out on the couch in his office. We need to know if there's anything we need to do right away, anoint him with olive oil or put garlic in his mouth or chant some prayer over his body."

"No, nothing like that. But he'll need to keep to a strict salt free diet." It was a miserable attempt to break the tension, but he was speaking more to himself than to the Chief of Staff, and he followed meekly as she led the way.

There was no question that President Torgeson was dead. His body was already cool to the touch, and the presence of death was so palpable that it stirred Norton's long dormant houngan abilities. Two bodyguards stood near the door, trying to look professional but only succeeding in appearing uncomfortable.

"Who else knows?"

Frakes glanced at the guards. "Besides the four of us, only Adamson at the CIA. I'll have to speak to the party leadership, of course. Thank God Torgeson is...was a bachelor."

"How about his personal physician?"

"Christian Scientist, remember? No doctor."

"Oh, right." Norton scratched his chin.

"So what do you need for the ceremony? Herbs? Magical artifacts? Drugs?"

Norton sighed. "Look, I think this whole thing is crazy under any circumstances, but even if I thought we might be able to pull it off, you've got the wrong man for the job. I've never raised a zombie; my talents aren't really strong enough for that kind of magic."

For just a second, it looked as though Frakes had let her shoulders slump. "You were the best chance we had."

"Maybe not. Look, I know a man who might be able to help. But you're not going to like this."

"There's nothing about this situation that I like, Norton, but I'm grasping for straws here."

"Nelson Djibwa."

That stopped her, at least for a few seconds. Nelson Djibwa was a thorn in the side of the Unionist Party. He'd run for office several times under their banner, twice winning a seat in the Louisiana legislature, twice defeated for a second term, primarily because the party refused to acknowledge him as a legitimate candidate.

"There must be someone else."

Norton nodded. "There probably is, but we have to move quickly here and he's the only one I know with the skills we need."

Frakes shook her head. "Then there's no choice but to make Torgeson's death public. God knows, I shudder to think what Curtis will do to this country, but having the President under the control of a man like Djibwa is too terrifying even to consider."

Norton shook his head. "You don't understand. I'm not suggesting that we have Djibwa raise the President. I'll perform the ceremony with his assistance. That way the zombie...I mean the President...will be bound to me personally. But we can draw on Djibwa's expertise." He paused to let that sink in. "You do realize that once raised, the President will be completely subservient to _my_ will, don't you?"

"Yes, I assumed that. Don't worry, Norton. We've checked you out thoroughly. I think you can be trusted to act responsibly, and I'll be the first to blow the whistle if my judgment proves faulty."

Norton experienced a brief glimpse of his future. "This is going to be a logistic nightmare. I'm scheduled to visit Europe next week, you realize."

"I've considered that. My staff is preparing press releases announcing a few changes in the administration."

"Changes?"

"Yes. Effective tomorrow morning, I am resigning my position as Chief of Staff in order to head President Torgeson's re-election campaign. A useless but necessary fiction, I'm afraid, but it will keep the public's attention centered until we come up with a new candidate. You'll have to resign as Secretary of State to take my old job. I know it's going to look like a step backward for you careerwise, but once I've had a chance to speak to a few members of the party leadership and explain the situation, I think you'll find you've accumulated a few favors."

Although Norton had mixed feelings, he realized the sense of what she was saying. And the possibility of being the Vice Presidential candidate in 2012 or 2016 was the unspoken undertext of her words. Who knew what might lie beyond?

"Then you'll bring in Djibwa?"

"I suppose we have no real choice. I just wonder what he'll want in return."

As it turned out, Djibwa wanted to be governor of Louisiana.

"Out of the question!" Frakes spoke angrily, while Norton, CIA director Adamson, and Unionist Party Chairman Estelle Novarro all regarded their slender, ebony skinned visitor with thinly disguised hostility. "The governorship is a public trust, not a commodity to be bartered."

Djibwa's face remained expressionless as he sat back in his chair, let his eyes roam around the walls of the White House conference room. "We are all sophisticated people here." His voice was deep and rich. "Is there time for us to indulge in the pretense of negotiation when we all know the truths of power?"

They all recognized that the Unionist Party enjoyed great popularity in Louisiana, had held the governor's mansion for three consecutive terms, and Governor Lavalier had already announced he would not seek a fourth term. An official endorsement would do more than legitimize Djibwa's candidacy, it would almost assure him election.

"You're asking a great price for your services," Novarro commented drily.

"You're asking for a very great service."

And in the end, they had no choice.

The ceremony itself didn't take long. Djibwa was ushered past security into the basement crisis room where the President's body currently lay in a cryogenic unit. Norton joined him there and the two men unpacked the ceremonial robes and artifacts of their craft while the President thawed under the watchful eyes of a CIA technician. Frakes had originally announced her intention to observe the process, but at the last minute demonstrated an uncharacteristic queasiness and excused herself.

"You're certain we can do this?" Norton was experiencing the old uncertainty, the lack of confidence which had marred his earlier attempts to master voodoo.

Djibwa's face and voice were neutral, but his eyes betrayed his contempt. "Your participation is not necessary and your doubts may interfere with my concentration."

At that moment, Norton desperately wanted to find some way to escape the situation, but there was no choice. Unless he was present and actively involved, Torgeson's reanimated body would be bound to Djibwa, an outcome they could not accept.

"My soul is at ease," he answered ritually, "and my will a tool for the shaping."

Djibwa continued to regard him doubtfully, but finally nodded and crossed to the body. "I believe we can start the ceremony now."

Two hours later, President Torgeson opened his eyes and rose obediently to his feet.

It took a full week before Norton began to believe they could get away with it. The President's hands had been covered with syntheskin gloves. Torgeson's grip was a little weak, but the President had never been one to press the flesh very much and they figured it would pass. Fortunately, his craggy face had never been particularly expressive and its present calm stolidity was actually a plus.

A synthesized television press conference went well. In fact, Torgeson's approval rating rose a full point the following day.

"We eliminated that damned hesitancy of his when he spoke," explained Frakes. "It was a subconscious signal of weakness and insincerity. How are you handling Curtis?"

"Just as we discussed. He's always been kept pretty isolated by Torgeson. Curtis understood why he was on the ticket and there was no love lost between the two men."

As Chief of Staff, Norton's constant proximity to the President had been legitimized, and since both men were unmarried, it was not considered particularly newsworthy when he moved into the guest wing of the White House on a more or less permanent basis. It was impractical to remain near at hand all the time, naturally, and the small group of people who knew the truth was slowly expanded until Torgeson was effectively insulated from discovery.

Norton saw the first reports of a double mutilation killing on the television in the rear of his limo the following morning. "Two unidentified men were discovered literally torn apart in a room on the fourteenth floor of the Sheridan Hotel," announced the newscaster. Norton, who'd been listening with only a fraction of his concentration, turned the volume up, remembering that Frakes had arranged for Djibwa to stay at that same hotel under an assumed name.

"Although neither man has been identified, the authorities are looking for Donald Cipher..." the screen faded and was replaced with a fair likeness of Nelson Djibwa, "...in connection with the incident. Although there has been no official confirmation, it is believed that Cipher was the guest registered in the room where the killings took place." When the story changed to a progress report on the Quebec Peace Talks, Norton turned the volume back down.

Frakes was sitting in his new office, her old one, when he arrived. Her face was deeply drawn and lacked its usually aggressiveness.

"What's going on?"

"We've lost Djibwa."

Norton frowned, then experienced an epiphany. "My God, you tried to have Djibwa sanctioned! I heard it on the radio on my way here."

"That's right. The casualties are two specialists I borrowed from Adamson. They were supposed to be quite expert at their jobs."

He suppressed a nervous laugh. "You might have mentioned this to me in advance. I could have told you it wouldn't work, and by trying and failing, you've made us a very powerful enemy."

She shrugged. "Did you really expect me to let him become Governor of Louisiana?"

Norton dropped onto the small couch and ran his fingers through his hair. "I suppose not, but I don't think you realize how powerful Djibwa is. He's not one of your everyday voodoo priests, you realize? If there is any single human being alive capable of carrying the mantle of Baron Samedi, it's Djibwa."

If Frakes was concerned, she concealed it well. "We underestimated him. It won't happen again."

"What are you planning to do?"

"Wait, at least for the moment. He'll surface somewhere. I have no doubt he realizes who was behind the attack. Most likely he'll show up with some media people, try to convince them that we've turned the President into a zombie." She laughed grimly. "No one will believe him, of course, and once we know where he is, we'll pick him up and slap him into the nearest sanitarium."

Norton shook his head. "That's not his style. It lacks...art. Voodoo is dependent upon rhythm, balance, integration of the soul into the flow of the universe. A direct confrontation would be inelegant."

Frakes made an inarticulate, impatient sound. "We'll integrate his soul into the universe, all right, and free him of all his worldly cares."

Several weeks later, there had still been no sign of Nelson Djibwa, and Frakes responded angrily whenever his name was raised.

"He'll want revenge, you realize," Norton told her on more than one occasion. "Not so much because of the attempt on his life, which he probably expected from the outset. But we reneged on our word, and that makes it imperative that he restore the equilibrium."

"Restore it? What can he do? There's no way he could reverse the spell on Torgeson, is there?"

Norton sighed, searching vainly for the right words. "It's not a spell, and no, he doesn't have any direct way to reverse the reanimation. That wouldn't be artful anyway. But he won't fold his tent and go home. Voodoo is a religion; he cannot refrain from acting without committing a dreadful sin."

At the same time, the elaborate pretense that Torgeson was still alive had settled down into a smooth routine. It was so smooth, in fact, that Norton felt occasional twinges of regret that it had become so easy to effectively scam the public.

Some public appearances could be handled by his doubles, who were accustomed to filling in for Torgeson when the President was committed to brief, boring ceremonies, convocations, and the like. None of them had been made privy to the truth. Norton had a staff member leak rumors to the media about a Quebec based assassination plot to explain the President's sharp curtailment of most public appearances and there had actually been a few editorials praising Torgeson for exposing himself at all.

Frakes ran the chimerical re-election campaign with her usual skill, and in fact Torgeson's approval rating had climbed steadily back to 54%, still low for an incumbent seeking a second term but considerably better than the 42% he had been polling at the time of his death. Part of this was because none of the Republicrats had yet emerged from the pack as a potential contender, but some of the improvement was surprising.

"Politics is a peculiar science," Frakes told Norton one evening. "I'm beginning to wonder if a dead candidate might be more viable than a live one."

"What do you mean?"

"Well, since Torgeson obviously doesn't give live speeches any more, we've been able to customize them for maximum impact. There are certain phrases, tones of voice, inflections, and patterns of sound and speech that are more reassuring than others. Torgeson was never particularly animated or articulate, but even though he moves slower than ever now, our enhancements have managed a net gain in his personal appeal. Our latest polls show that people describe him as calm, controlled, fatherly, and strong willed." She shook her head. "Controlled he is, but strong willed?" Her voice cracked a little toward the end.

"How's Bergeron coming along?" Stan Bergeron had been chosen secretly by the Unionist Party leadership to be the real candidate in the next election. The strategy was for him to provide a credible but unthreatening challenge in the primaries, thereby keeping Curtis in line, later to be nominated at the convention after Torgeson withdrew "for reasons of health".

"He's doing all the right things, but he's still slipping in the polls. You saw how he did in New Hampshire."

"Eight percent."

"Right. But that's because everyone assumes Torgeson will be the nominee."

The primaries rolled past, each awarding Torgeson an overwhelming percentage of the delegates. His approval rating nationwide rose to 61% by the end of April, 66% by the end of May. Dorothy Baldwin now seemed certain to secure the Republicrat nomination, but she was trailing Torgeson in the polls by over thirty points.

Three days prior to the California primary, Stan Bergeron was killed in a plane crash while flying to a rally in Oakland. Torgeson had long since sewn up the unofficial nomination, of course, but now there was no viable candidate waiting to step into his shoes...except for the Vice President, Samuel Curtis.

"What are we going to do?" Norton had called Frakes at home, on their secure line.

"It looks like we'll have to run Torgeson for re-election."

"Run Torgeson! Are you out of your mind?" But he didn't argue for long. It had all begun to make some kind of bizarre sense. Or perhaps he'd been living in the political world so long that nothing surprised him any more.

Norton was eating by himself in a small dining room in the White House when one of his aides rushed in and turned on the television.

"Dorothy Baldwin has been assassinated!" She was nearly breathless with excitement. And they both watched several replays of the taped assault, Baldwin just finishing her remarks about the state of the economy, raising her arms high above her head, then the series of sharp reports, a popping noise that didn't sound at all dangerous. Baldwin's head snapped back as the first round struck high on her forehead, then dropped out of sight as those surrounding her exploded into kaleidoscopic panic.

But Dorothy Baldwin was not dead, they discovered a few hours later. She had received only a single, glancing wound along the side of her head, and would be recovered enough to resume her campaign within a few days.

When she made her first televised appearance five days later, one side of her face swathed with bandages, it was Norton who called Frakes to an emergency meeting at the White House.

"What's the problem?" The strain of recent events was clearly taking its toll. Her face was drawn, hair in disarray, and there were tension cracks in her voice.

"Just watch this." He replayed Baldwin's press conference on the overhead monitor, first at normal speed, then again in slow motion.

"Notice anything?"

"She looks a little pale, but considering how close she came to being killed, I suppose that's understandable."

"Now watch this." On a second monitor, he played back a tape of the assassination tape, then hit pause at the point where Baldwin's head snapped back. "If you'll look closely, you can just see where the round struck her forehead."

"It looks pretty bad from that angle, but the bullet was deflected by her skull. A very lucky woman; she'll be a formidable opponent in the fall."

Norton shook his head. "Not lucky at all. The first shot went directly into the skull."

Frakes frowned. "Impossible. If it was that serious, they'd never have been able to get her back on her feet so quickly, if she survived at all."

"Torgeson is back on his feet, and he's dead."

Frakes shifted uncomfortably. "I don't understand what you're trying to say."

Norton rewound the tape of the press conference and started it again. "Watch the crowd this time, particularly the members of Baldwin's personal staff." He waited for a frame he'd examined closely for almost an hour, then froze the picture. "Two rows back and slightly to the left."

A few seconds later, Frakes drew her breath in sharply. "Djibwa!"

"Right."

"Do you suppose he told Baldwin what we've done, and that she believed him?"

"No, I don't think that at all. In fact, I think Djibwa engineered the successful assassination of the Republicrat nominee for President."

"Engineered? You mean, he had Baldwin killed? But why?" But even as she spoke, her eyes widened.

"I told you he'd find a way to strike back artistically. Baldwin has already announced that she'll be reducing her schedule of appearances. No one will fault her for it under the circumstances. My guess is that we'll find out Baldwin is in the midst of a major reorganization of her staff, and the only ones who will survive are those Djibwa can bend to his will, or who aren't in a position to spot what's really going on."

"Oh my God." Frakes seemed sincerely shaken. "And we have no choice now but to run Torgeson against her. Whatever happens, no matter which candidate wins, we're facing another four years with a zombie as President. This is a complete disaster."

"Maybe."

Frakes turned to face him, her composure cracking for the first time since Norton had known her. "What do you mean?"

"Frankly, Jennifer, I doubt most people will even notice a difference."

As it turned out, Norton was right.

DUMB GENIUS

Chester Baker's downfall began the day he found the collection of science fiction stories on a shelf in the utility closet at Fermi's Electronics shop. Chester was a valued employee, the best after hours cleaning person the store had ever employed. A little too good, as it turned out. He finished his duties early almost every evening, and although he read slowly, sounding out each word, he was persistent enough to stick with it for the several weeks he needed to finish the slim paperback.

Unfortunately, Chester was more than entertained; he was also inspired. Here at last was a way for him to escape his low paying job. Chester Baker had decided to become a master criminal.

Chester's academic and social deficiencies were balanced by an uncanny affinity for electronic and mechanical devices. Several of the "adjustments" he'd made to appliances in his cramped, three room apartment would have made him very wealthy if he'd known to approach someone in the right line of business. But Chester really didn't see anything extraordinary about a television set that displayed four channels simultaneously on a partitioned screen, or a stove that worked perfectly with one tenth the usual current, or a microwave that cooled as well as heated.

It required only a few stolen hours and some misappropriated equipment from Fermi's stockroom to make his first scheme practical. The initial test runs of the matter transmitter were less than satisfactory, and if the store cat hadn't jumped onto the transfer plate at precisely the right moment, Chester might have abandoned his plans prematurely. But the cat jumped, disappeared, and reappeared at the focus point between two storage cabinets, minus her collar and distinctly upset. The missing collar lay on the transfer plate, and after several minutes rumination, Chester concluded correctly that matter transmission only worked with living things. But that was fine with him.

There was a jewelry store directly across the street. Chester borrowed a tape measure and painstakingly calculated the distance, then meticulously adjusted the controls of his invention. The store closed at ten o'clock the following evening, but just to be safe, Chester waited until midnight before firing up his equipment. Five minutes later he stood on the transfer plate and felt a very mild tingling sensation that caused him to close his eyes for a few seconds.

When he opened them, Chester was inside Prestige Jewelers. He was also stark naked. That didn't bother him particularly, since there was no one around to notice, and he spent the next several minutes filling a large box with colorful but not particularly expensive watches, bracelets, and broaches. A large display of diamond rings tempted him, but they were in a locked display case with its own alarm system, and he reluctantly turned away. Chester figured he could make several trips before dawn, pack everything in the trunk of his aging Volkswagen, and be gone before anyone arrived to sound the alarm.

It was at just that moment that Chester realized he'd neglected to think things through. Although he'd been projected past the electric eyes that guarded every door and window, there was no way to return without setting them off. He glanced out the front window toward the police station, only a block away, and considered his options. Just possibly he could burst through the door, cross the street, and disappear inside Fermi's before anyone showed up to investigate. But the box of stolen goods would slow him down and he didn't dare risk it. Reluctantly he set his loot aside, drew a deep breath, and burst through the door.

The alarms went crazy and the rough ground hurt his feet, but Chester locked his eyes on the electronics shop, ignored the pain, and raced forward, not daring to look toward the police station. He reached the front door and automatically reached for the set of keys hanging from his belt.

But the keys, along with belt and trousers, were already inside. Chester's teeth were chattering with more than the cold as a nearby siren wound up to a shriek. He made it to the adjacent alley just before the headlights of the patrol car swept the main street, hustled down to the rear entrance. That door was locked as well, but the alarms at Fermi were off and Chester used a large stone to break the glass. Back inside, he leaned against the outside wall, struggling to catch his breath, and only moved when the chill night air began to invade the shop.

Ten minutes later, fully dressed, Chester used a spare pane of glass to repair the rear door. Then he returned to his makeshift workshop and disassembled the matter transmitter into its constituent pieces, returning them to the stock room. He had a better idea.

Chester's time machine was rather limited. He could not travel into the future at all, and only backwards for a few hours. The device was actually quite small; he could carry a complete unit in his pants pocket quite readily. At first he was afraid that his second invention suffered the same fault as the first, because the time machine itself remained in the present. Fortunately, it appeared that matter was somehow attached to its own timeline. Precisely ten minutes after the field was turned on, the effect ended and whatever had been transported, organic or not, returned to normal.

He resolved to test it the very next day.

The sales clerk at Prestige Jewelers eyed him skeptically when he entered. The abortive burglary had made the staff edgy and suspicious. Chester had been sitting in his car for several minutes, waiting until there were enough customers in the store to occupy the staff. Nervously rubbing the bulge in his pants pocket, he almost froze when the clerk met his eyes, but she turned back to the customer she was assisting. Breathing deeply to calm his nerves, he walked slowly toward the rear of the store, pretending to look at the items in the display cases. There were a half dozen other customers in the store, and he had a few uneasy moments when it appeared that he would never be entirely unnoticed.

Shopping patterns shifted and he was suddenly unobserved. Chester thrust a hand into his pocket, withdrew the time machine, and pressed a stud. Everything grew blurry for a few seconds, the light faded toward darkness, and then reality came back. He found himself standing in Prestige Jewelers, but now there were neither customers nor employees to see him. Only the security lights were on, and his hands were empty. The time machine remained back in the present, currently his future.

Chester had given the situation more thought this time. He walked directly to the diamond display and waited, studying his wristwatch for several minutes. Satisfied, he broke the glass, selected several of the most expensive, and put them in his pocket. The alarms went off immediately, of course, but thirty seconds later his ten minute journey through time came to an end and he and the stolen jewelry disappeared.

His vision blurred and brightened and he was back in the present. The time machine was in his hand, and a reassuring bulge in his pocket reassured him that this time he'd been successful. Now all that was necessary was to walk out of the store.

The diamond display was exactly as he remembered it, which puzzled Chester considerably. Could they have repaired and restocked it so quickly? It bothered him, but he was too nervous to worry about it just now. Ignoring the sales clerk who offered to assist him, Chester walked steadily to the front door, then outside, his heart beating desperately as he worried that somehow he'd overlooked something, that the police would be waiting to arrest him.

But they weren't. He got into his Volkswagen, started the engine, drove two blocks down the street, then pulled over to the curb. There was no one around, so he removed the diamonds from his pocket. They were beautiful, he thought, and worth a lot of money. He hadn't worked out exactly how he would sell them yet, but the glow of triumph made him confident he'd work that out as well.

The diamonds suddenly shimmered and disappeared, drawn back to their own time by the ten minute limit. Chester blinked, his brow furrowed, his elation slipping away. "That's not fair!" He protested weakly.

He disassembled the time machine an hour later.

Chester's third invention was a replicator. It was so simple that it only took one evening to build, and he couldn't understand why it hadn't been done before. In appearance it resembled a balance scale, with a round plate on either side. Once connected to a power source, it vibrated slightly, and when Chester dropped a piece of copper wire onto one plate and pressed the "On" button, it was immediately duplicated on the other. He experimented with several small articles, nuts and bolts, a chunk of his chocolate bar, the stub of a pencil, before feeling confident that it worked as he'd hoped.

There was a single twenty dollar bill in his wallet, all that remained of his meager paycheck. Chester carefully folded it in two so that none of the edges would project beyond the circumference of the first plate. Then he pressed the button. A twenty dollar bill, neatly folded, appeared on the other. He removed the newcomer and pressed the button again, and a third bill appeared.

Within an hour Chester had accumulated a sore thumb and several thousand dollars, all neatly folded and gathered into a cardboard box. The joy of creation dimmed at last and he sat back in his chair, contemplating the newfound fortune. He'd quit his job, of course; he'd never have to work again. A little electricity was all he needed to create more money whenever he needed some. The realization that he would never again have to take broom in hand made him almost giddy with excitement and he leaped to his feet, danced a little jig, and knocked over his box of money.

Even that little mishap did nothing to spoil his mood, and Chester dropped to his knees, collecting the wayward twenties with both hands, laughing hysterically as he poured them back into the box.

The laughter stopped quite abruptly when Chester looked closely at his money. There was something odd about Andrew Jackson. He couldn't quite figure it out until his eyes dropped lower and he saw the caption. It was reversed, a mirror image of the original bill.

Chester burned the bogus money in the incinerator and stamped the replicator into junk, never realizing he could simply have used one of the bogus bills as the original to create an equally large pile of correctly oriented cash.

It was a week before Chester could gather the energy to try again, but there were still a few ideas he'd read about that might work. His next effort was less ambitious in effect, but required much more effort to carry off. But eventually his prototype tested out, and a full scale version followed a day later. Determined not to fail again, Chester built a cloak of electronic wires and a helmet made of copper mesh. Eight "C" batteries attached to his belt were the power source and the wires were the transmitters.

Wrapped in the cloak, wearing the helmet, Chester drove to the parking lot behind Fermi's the following afternoon. There he waited until he was sure no one was around, then stepped out of the car and turned on his invention. There was a brief flash of light and Chester Baker disappeared from sight, startling a pair of birds who'd been watching him from a nearby tree.

Chester was invisible.

He couldn't even see himself, a side effect that he hadn't quite gotten used to. Walking was a real problem, particularly over uneven ground, and when he reached the street, he hesitated at the curb. But this time he was determined to see things through. He would enter Fermi's, wait until the clerk's back was turned, then grab whatever was easiest. Once inside the aura of his suit, the stolen merchandise would be invisible as well, and Chester could saunter back outside without anyone being the wiser.

But the curb made him nervous. If he fell, he might break one of the circuits and lose part or all of his invisibility. Tentatively, he felt his way with one foot, then followed with the second. He concentrated harder than he'd ever done before, determined to get it right. Watching the ground intently, he began shuffling across the street.

The bus driver who ran Chester down never saw him, of course.

HAIR APPARENT

Melanie read the framed certificate for the fourth time since seating herself in Madame Estelle's waiting room. "ESTELLE BARON IS DULY CERTIFIED TO PRACTICE WITCHCRAFT IN ACCORDANCE WITH ALL LOCAL LAWS AND REGULATIONS". It bore the imprimatur of the American Wiccan Association.

"It'll be all right," she whispered to herself. "She's a professional. It's just like going to a doctor."

Indeed, it had been her regular physician, Dr. Chalmers, who had sent her here.

"I've made an appointment for you with a specialist, Ms Rule. I've referred several other patients to her in the past and they've all been completely satisfied."

But a witch? Melanie shook her head. She knew intellectually that the AWA had scientifically proven the efficacy of its treatment, but it had always seemed remote and inapplicable to herself, like acupuncture.

She grabbed a magazine from the table, paged past an editorial condemning the life insurance industry's adamant refusal to pay for the lifting of curses. A sidebar proclaimed in bold print that "the contention that curses are criminal acts and therefore not health issues is specious at best".

"Ms Rule?"

Melanie glanced up. The apprentice who had taken her name when she first arrived had returned. A patch bearing a pair of stylized snakes coiled around a broomstick was sewed on one shoulder and over the breast pocket.

"Yes?"

"Madame Estelle will see you now. This way please."

The moment had come. Melanie felt a sudden thrust of nausea, suppressed it. She needed help, after all, and this might be the only place she could get it.

"So what seems to be the problem?"

Madame Estelle was not at all what Melanie had expected. No

exotic clothing, for example. She wore a tailored business suit and her pepper grey hair was neat and attractive. The office could have been that of a lawyer if it hadn't been for the crystal ball bookends, the elaborate zodiac tapestry adorning one wall, and the beautifully constructed replica of Stonehenge set in a glass case beside the desk.

Melanie tried to speak, couldn't get the words out.

"Your first time seeing a Wiccan?" Madame Estelle smiled and turned away, giving Melanie time to recover her composure. "I imagine I'm not at all what you expected, either. Hollywood still insists on the old familiar caricature despite the efforts of the Wiccan Defense League."

"I'm sorry. I didn't mean to be rude. Dr. Chalmers referred me to you because he couldn't find a physical cause for my illness and it's clearly not psychosomatic."

"And just what exactly is wrong with you?" Melanie hesitated and Madame Estelle made an impatient sound. "Out with it, girl. I don't read minds, you know. Not my specialty."

With a conscious effort to keep her voice level, Melanie explained her problem. "My hair won't stop growing. I mean, it won't grow at a normal rate. Two or three inches a day, usually, sometimes even more."

The witch raised her eyebrows but her expression was otherwise neutral. "An unusual curse, if that's what it is. Some might find it a blessing."

Melanie shook her head vigorously. "Surely you know how long it takes to wash and dry that much hair. And I can't afford to see the hairdresser every three or four days. Can you help me?"

Madame Estelle nodded. "I think so. But first we'll need to do some tests. My apprentice will take an auragram and we'll need an ectoplasmic sample for testing." She paused thoughtfully. "And I'll want you to give some thought to what might have happened in the weeks preceding the onset of this condition. Any change in your living habits, new job, new lover, new enemies, that sort of thing. The curse is a symptom, you realize? The root cause must be addressed or you'll simply find yourself with a new disorder, hives, a wen, or something even less pleasant."

"I can't imagine..."

Madame Estelle raised a hand. "Don't think about it just now. You'll need to be calm for the auragram."

Melanie left the office in a state of some confusion. On the one hand, the brisk professional manner with which she'd been treated was reassuring, as was Madame Estelle's evident self confidence. On the other hand, neither having her picture taken with a peculiar looking camera using a blacklight flashbulb nor watching the apprentice painlessly sample a wispy white substance that seemed to seep from the palm of Melanie's hand had seemed quite normal.

But neither was waking up with hair down to her shoulderblades every morning.

She reached into her pocket, checked to be certain the small pamphlet was still there. Madame Estelle had handed it to her just before she'd left the office.

"It's a book of charms," she'd explained. "Just before bed I want you to chant three mantras, and call me in the morning."

Melanie spent the evening lying on her couch, trying to think of anyone she might have annoyed recently. The curse had only been active for four weeks, and little in her life had changed in the period immediately preceding. She'd finished the preliminary engineering for the new distillation column at Vesuvius Chemical, but that was only one of several routine projects she'd been dealing with for months. There'd been no arguments, her staff seemed happy, and there hadn't been any serious rivalries at the firm in over a year.

There was a new CAD operator, Peter Reynolds, unusually shy but friendly. At first she'd thought he was interested in Carla, the purchasing manager, but now she was pretty certain he was working up his courage to ask her out instead, and Melanie had already decided to say yes. But she hadn't rejected him and couldn't believe he bore her any malice.

"This is ridiculous." She tossed aside the legal pad on which she'd been making notes. "I'm not mad at anyone and I can't imagine why anyone would be mad at me."

But in the morning, her hair had grown another four inches.

"The results of your tests were quite interesting. Could you come in to see me this afternoon at, say, three o'clock."

Melanie nodded, then spoke aloud into the phone. "Sure, I'll be there. Thank you, Madame Estelle." So far, no one at work knew of her problem, and she didn't plan to explain her absence except in the vaguest of terms. She had sick leave coming, and if Vesuvius balked at that, she'd take some of her accumulated vacation.

Melanie left at lunch, which provided enough time for another trim.

"I've never seen anything exactly like this." Madame Estelle pointed at the silhouette mounted on her wall. It was a human form, the outline filled with swirling greens and yellows, except for the head, which displayed a faint superimposed latticework of red and a cap of vivid blue.

"Is that me?"

"That's your auragram, yes. By interpreting the colors and patterns, we can often determine where the imbalances lie. The normal colors of life are hues of green and yellow, as you see. Anger, distress, hatred, any strong negative emotion shows up as red."

"Is that the curse then?" Melanie pointed to the lightning shaped red lines.

"I think not. It is too fragile and undirected. What you see there is probably your own fear and concern. No, this is the interesting feature." And she pointed to the blue spot, which covered the top of the skull. "Curses are, generally, manifestations of black magic, and therefore show up as black spots, much as cancer might in an X-Ray. Considering the location, which I suspect we will find entirely covers the scalp, I feel certain this is the source of your problem."

"Can you get rid of it?"

"Yes, I believe so. But as I told you before, we must cure the disease rather than treat a symptom. Have you thought of anything which might have led to this situation?"

She shook her head. "Nothing at all. I can't imagine why anyone would dislike me so much..."

Madame Estelle shook her head. "It is not, perhaps, that they dislike you. This coloration is all wrong for a vengeful curse. I think you've encountered a latent."

"A latent? I don't understand."

The witch paused a moment, then pointed to the encased Stonehenge. "There was and is no magic in these stones, Ms Rule. Nor is there anything magical in crystal balls, Tarot cards, or most of the other paraphernalia of Wicca. Witchcraft is the power of the will, and the instruments we use are merely symbols which held us to concentrate and achieve our purpose. But it is possible to achieve the same thing without any of the ritual, even without knowing what one is doing, if the ability lies within."

Melanie thought about that. "You mean, someone might have cursed me by accident?"

"That's exactly what I think. There was no evil intent here, or the aura would show black. Instead, it is blue."

"And what does blue signify?"

"Friendship, admiration, love." Madame Estelle sighed. "So I ask you again, has anything happened recently which might have changed the way someone thinks about you?"

Realization came suddenly. "Peter!"

Madame Estelle was thoughtfully silent after Melanie finished describing her relationship, such as it was, with Peter Reynolds. Melanie waited for as long as she could, then blurted out her concern. "Are you saying Peter is some kind of witch?"

"Not in the ordinary sense, perhaps, though with the proper training, he could probably become a master warlock. This much power from someone unskilled in the Arts is quite rare."

"But I still don't understand why he'd do this to me, even unconsciously. I thought he liked me."

"He undoubtedly does. I told you, the aura would be black if it were otherwise, conscious act or not. I believe his unacknowledged motives are...well...benevolent."

"Benevolent?" Melanie reached up to touch her hair, which was already perceptibly longer than when she'd left The Clipjoint an hour before.

"Yes. I suspect your admiring friend thinks you'd be more attractive if you let your hair grow longer. And his unconscious mind is trying to help."

Melanie digested that, nodded. "All right, this all sounds crazy to me, but I'm obviously out of my depth. What do I do?"

"Nothing for the moment. Come back Friday afternoon. I'll have the answer for you then."

Wednesday her hair grew three inches, Thursday only two, but Friday morning it regained lost ground and gained five inches in six hours. Melanie showed up for her appointment forty five minutes early.

"So can you help me?"

"As I said I would. Take these." Melanie accepted two vials.

"What do I do with them?"

"The orange is a shampoo. Use it all up in a single washing, as many rinses as it takes. Work the solution into your scalp vigorously and let it stand for a full minute before each rinse. That should return the growth rate to normal. I warn you the odor is quite unpleasant. But wait for at least an hour afterward before shampooing it normally."

"And this?" Melanie held up the blue vial.

"That's the true cure. There are two tablets in it. You must get your admirer to consume them both entirely as they are precisely measured. It will reverse his fondness for long hair and prevent any recurrence of your condition."

Melanie twisted off the cap, sniffed a mildly repugnant odor. "What is it?"

"You don't really want to know. Finely ground rat hair is its most savory component. There's a bit of an unpleasant taste, but it should be masked by, say, dissolving them in a strong cup of coffee."

Peter positively blushed when she offered to bring him coffee from the canteen, and he asked her to dinner while he was drinking it. Melanie accepted, but watched carefully to be certain he drained his cup. She was smiling when she returned to her office.

Madame Estelle looked forward to her Coven's bowling night avidly, even more so this month because she wanted to tell Simone about the strange case she'd treated this past week. But to her surprise, and growing alarm, it turned out Simone had dealt with the identical complaint a day earlier. And had treated it in the same fashion.

Peter Reynolds felt wonderful. For weeks he'd been trying to gather the nerve to ask either Melanie Rule or Carla Henderson out on a date, and today they'd both approached him. He hadn't really wanted a second cup of coffee, but Carla had been so insistent.

Melanie woke up feeling wonderful. The dinner had been superb, both the food and the company. Peter was really clever and funny once he'd relaxed. This could be the one, she thought, then dismissed it as more than slightly premature. We hardly know each other, she thought.

It was Saturday so she didn't have to get up, but her bladder demanded attention. She rolled out of bed, fumbled her way into slippers, and staggered to the bathroom.

She didn't start screaming until she looked into the mirror and discovered she was completely bald.

THE DAYLIGHT VAMPIRE

Roger's eyes popped open as the alarm sounded and he stared directly into the bank of fluorescent lights he had installed in his new hiding place. In one of the rented room, the ready light glowed on an expensive battery backup system. The fluorescents themselves were on two separate circuits, a modification for which he had paid the landlord handsomely. A dozen lamps were scattered about the room as well, all fitted with extended life light bulbs and all glowing brilliantly.

He glanced at his wristwatch, confirmed that it was well after dawn, and sat up, drawing several deep breaths before climbing over the rim of the oversized crib which he had lined with his birthsoil, carefully dug from the grounds of the house in which he had been born nearly two centuries earlier. Stretching languorously to relieve the tension in his cramped muscles, Roger prepared to meet the new day.

Cautiously, he crossed to the nearest window, cautiously lifting one corner of the slatted blinds so that he could peer outside. The alley six floors below was flooded by the summer sun. With a sigh of relief, he drew the blind completely and allowed the restorative, natural sunlight to flow over his body, suffusing it with strength. He felt renewed vigor as the healing rays soaked into his flesh, inflating his muscles to more than human capacity, accelerating the metabolic processes that made him virtually immune to disease and physical damage. Within moments he felt fully fit and ready to venture forth in pursuit of today's prey.

Roger Henderson was a daylight vampire.

He emerged onto the street several minutes later, tasting the air with his superhuman senses. Already, the sense of fullness was making him uncomfortable, a swelling that started in his breast, progressed through the throat and into the underside of his jaw. It was imperative that he find a victim, but it would not do to strike so close to his resting place. Already there was danger. He could sense the presence of enemies, human being aware of his preternatural abilities and determined to bring them to an end.

Up until recently, he had been able to cross directly through Peterson Park into the downtown, but urban renewal at the far end of the city had altered the water table, and the running brooks that meandered through the park had backed up into a network of still pools. Barred by his nature from crossing stagnant water, Roger was now forced to detour around the park and approach the city through the warehouse district.

He walked briskly, enjoying the smooth flow of his muscles, the beat of the sun on his forehead. It was a glorious day and he felt invulnerable, immortal, and irresistible. Such over confidence was dangerous for one such as he, and he strove to hold tight rein on his emotions as he passed along a line of decaying buildings, emerging into a broad public square filled with makeshift wooden booths, wheeled carts, open-backed pickup trucks, and garishly painted vans. This was the unofficial farmers' market, and already several hundred prospective customers were milling about, looking for fresh produce at less than retail prices.

The glands in Roger's neck throbbed lustily as he walked among them, an intense pressure whose ultimate relief would be a sensual gratification beyond the most exquisite sexual pleasures of ordinary human beings. The aching sensation was paradoxically enjoyable; he knew from experience that the longer he prolonged the anticipation, the more rewarding would be the release.

He stopped at the rear of a green Volkswagen mini-van, his nostrils twitching.

"Excuse me, would you have any fresh garlic?"

The man who turned to wait on him had a particularly ugly scar down one cheek, a disfigurement that pleased Roger because of its uniqueness. He took great pains to make his purchases from different vendors each time, thereby reducing the likelihood that he would be remembered.

"Whole or chopped?" The voice was a disinterested monotone.

"Whole."

Without changing expression, the young man held up strings of uncut garlic and quoted a price. Roger paid him and accepted his purchase in a paper bag. It smelled wondrous, but he would dine later. His immediate concern was to relieve the incredible pressures still mounting with him.

He left the market square and passed along a row of department stores. They were still closed at this early hour, although there was activity within a few, employees making changes in the attire, position, or surroundings of window manikins, a few maintenance people vacuuming or dusting. As a rule, Roger avoided going inside. There were too many people about to choose a victim in that environment, and there tended to be a lot of mirrors. Few were likely to recognize the significance of the strange double image that was his reflection, but it only took one knowledgeable person in the right place at the wrong time to endanger his existence.

Briskly, he passed through the shopping district, progressed through several blocks of professional offices, the buildings gradually declining in size and rising in age. The level of pedestrian traffic fluctuated as well, becoming much thinner as he reached his favorite prowling ground. The highway overpass towered overhead and the constant rumbling of vehicles passing above provided the soundtrack for the drama about to unfold.

Roger stood at the intersection of two infrequently traveled streets. The decaying buildings stretching away on either side were decorated with garish neon signs, some hanging over the sidewalk, others mounted in windows. The majority advertised a variety of bars with little to distinguish among them. There were as well a couple of flophouses, a second hand book store, a bail bond office, two pawn shops, and a small delicatessen, plus further businesses beyond. A handful of street people were walking aimlessly up and down, and another handful were sitting or lying in doorways, most of them asleep.

Two incongruously well-dressed men in gray raincoats stood half a block away, talking quietly but animatedly. One of them looked familiar but Roger couldn't place him.

Roger bided his time, choosing his victim with care. When his selection was complete, he stepped forward, crossing the distance from the elderly man whose faltering footsteps seemed each a major accomplishment.

"Excuse me, sir. Could you tell me how to find Victor Street?" The pressure pounded insistently in his throat.

"Eh?" With bleary eyes, the man raised his head. Roger noted with satisfaction the matted hair, heavily lidded eyes, unshaven jowls, palsied shaking hands, trembling lip. He repeated his question, moving closer.

"S'over there somewhere," the man waved vaguely toward the south.

"Could you show me? If you have the time, that is." Roger did his best to smile winningly. "I'd be happy to pay you for your time."

Frowning, his companion made a conscious if ineffectual effort to establish some air of dignity. "How much?"

"Oh, I think ten dollars would be fair, don't you?"

Naked avarice sparked in those flagging eyes and Roger felt an easing of his own internal pressure. Too soon, he thought. Let's mnpt be premature.

Ten minutes later, he pushed the old man behind a scraggly hedgerow in what was at one time one of the stylish sections of the old city. His prey's outraged cry of protest was cut off as Roger pounced, enveloping him with his own body. His inner need swelled to the bursting point at the contact and at last he truly fed.

When he had finished, Roger stood up, staring down at his latest victim. The derelict was sleeping comfortably and fresh color suffused formerly pallid cheeks. The trembling had gone now and his breathing was deep, even, healthy. In a matter of minutes, he had shed years.

Roger's reaction was a refreshing weakness, an almost sexual peacefulness. The pressure had dissipated and he knew he would be at ease until the following morning. He opened his bag and began breaking off garlic cloves and eating them, drawing energy from their sustaining power.

At that moment, the two well-dressed gentlemen attacked.

They had clearly come prepared. The first held up a small American flag, advancing toward Roger with steady steps. He reacted to this symbol of temporal authority by hissing warningly and retreating a step, arms raised to shield his eyes.

"Stand where you are, foul creature!" his enemy thunder. "Your time is due!"

Although he longed to advance and knock the hated image from the man's hand, Roger knew that he was vulnerable to its inherent power. With an inarticulate cry of rage, he spun on his heel, prepared to flee headlong, but now the other man stepped into view, brandishing blank IRS forms 1040 in each hand. Their presence was enough to cause him acute pain even over the intervening distance.

"Your foul reign of terror is at an end!" continued the first man. "We have suspected your presence among us for some time, and now we have seen for ourselves the evil you have brought to our city. You have provided sustenance to those who should perish for the benefit of society."

Roger's eyes darted back and forth between the two, who were obviously Republicans. He could go neither forward nor back. To his right loomed the stained, graffiti covered wall of an abandoned factory; to his left the undisciplined growth of privet behind which he had hoped to remain unobserved. Only one option remained.

Roger was not so easily defeated. After two centuries of relieving his unearthly satiation on the fringes of human society, he had learned to be prepared for every situation. By the time his two assailants had realized what was happening, it was too late to react. His body shrank in on itself, his folded arms blending into more graceful shapes. Within seconds, while the two men raced forward in a desperate attempt to prevent his escape, Roger had transformed himself into a beautiful, oversized dove.

His wings lifted him off into the bright morning sunlight.

Roger woke in the night, disoriented, certain that something was wrong. He spread his arms, searching for the reassuring coldness of his birthsoil. Without success.

His eyes snapped open and panic swept in. The room was in virtually complete darkness. Both banks of fluorescents were extinguished, as were all but one of the other lamps. Instead of resting in the womb of his crib, he was lying on his back in the middle of the floor two meters away. Weakness sapped his muscles and he was torn between the desire to restore the precious light and the need to crawl back into his crib, to touch that soil once more and draw upon its power. The latter urge prevailed.

Staggering to his feet, Roger lurched across the room, reaching out to grab the side of the crib.

And jumped back with alacrity as pain shot through the palms of both hands.

The stimulus helped disperse some of the fog that cluttered his brain, however, and he was able to concentrate his preternatural vision even in this dim light and discover the source of that painful repulsion.

Someone had systematically affixed postage stamps strategically across the outer rim of the crib. He was forever barred from returning there!

"That's right, monster, we've trapped you at last." One of the men who had attacked him earlier stepped out into the pool of light cast by the single lamp.

"And this time there'll be no escape." The second voice was raspy, a sound that he recognized. Now he remembered where he had seen the familiar looking man before; he had been in the lobby of this very building, speaking to the desk clerk a day or two earlier.

Obviously they had been pursuing him for some time.

"I may be weakened but I'm still a match for the two of you," Roger assured them in a voice that shook with emotion, drawing what strength he could from the warm radiance from the single lamp.

"That remains to be seen," the first man contradicted him, and without a further word he turned and kicked over the lamp.

As the light vanished, Roger screamed, a deep, soulful cry of pain and hopelessness. He fell senseless to the floor.

There was no way to ascertain how much time had passed between that moment and the one in which Roger regained consciousness. Lying on his back, he initially thought that the encounter in his room had been a particularly unpleasant dream, but his languor remained and there was no sense of the presence of his birthsoil. As a matter of fact, when he tried to move his limbs to search for some trace of that restoring element, he discovered that he was totally immobilized.

Then he noticed the chanting. There were two voices, one reciting the Pledge of Allegiance in a singsong, the individual words losing their meaning, sublimated to the greater significance of its ritual value. The second voice seemed to be less certain of his text, stumbled over words and phrases, delivering what was a warped but identifiable variation of the Constitution of the United States.

These were no amateurs. He had fallen into the hands of professional conservatives. There could be no escape.

The chanting came to an end. The two figure approached and a flashlight clicked on, throwing enough light to allow Roger to see that he lay spread-eagled under a sheltering tarpaulin tied between a telephone pole and two tree trunks.

"Perish, evil spirit, and trouble this world no more." With those words the two men quickly untied the tarpaulin and pulled it away.

Pale moonlight washed across the ground and over his body. Where its limpid radiance struck his flesh, small crystals formed, growing in size, multiplying, spreading under his clothing. Roger began to thrash and squirm as his body was transformed, but the process was incredibly rapid, starting in his extremities and rushing toward conjunction in his abdomen and chest. His head was the last to go and when it finally froze solid, his expression was one of defiant derision.

The two men watched in fascinated horror as the crystalline ice cracked and fell away, steaming in the moonlight. Roger's flesh seemed renewed, unblemished, features changing with increasing rapidity as the process continued. Adulthood sloughed away in seconds as Roger progressed back through adolescence to childhood, to infancy, growing ever less massive as his unnatural existence came to an end. Finally, nothing remained, nothing visible in any case; it was actually several seconds longer before the last cell separated into its primal constituents.

The creature known as Roger Henderson had passed from the world of humanity, which was now free to exploits its weaker members without hindrance. The horror was over.

LOVE CHARM

Paul Sheldon stood beside the grave of his late wife Evelyn, his thoughts lost in time, his fingers idly caressing the amulet he had spent four years and nearly all of his savings to obtain. He had remained nearly motionless in that place for over thirty minutes now, and his companion stirred restlessly as he leaned against a maple tree several yards away.

"Paul," he said at last. "We really should be going now. It's getting dark and they'll be chasing people out so they can lock the gates for the night."

Sheldon gave no indication that he had heard, other than a convulsive tightening of his grip on the amulet.

When it was clear that there would be no response, John Travers sighed and stood clear of the tree, brushing the hair back from his forehead wearily. "Paul, isn't there some way I can talk you out of this? It won't work, you know. Surely somewhere inside you realize that. You're obsessed by your grief and it's affected your rationality. I know you can't accept that, but at least entertain the possibility that I know what I'm talking about."

Sheldon's eyes narrowed at his old friend's words, but he never raised his eyes from their regard of the grass that masked his wife's resting place, never answered.

Travers swore under his breath, took several nervous steps away, then spun on his heel to face the other man.

"Why do you insist on doing this to yourself? Indulging delusions like this won't do your sanity any good, you know. You've already lost your livelihood, your home, your friends – most of them anyway, your future if you keep on this way. Even if your magic charm worked, would it be worth all of that?"

Slowly Sheldon released a long held breath, allowed his shoulders to relax slightly, and shifted one foot.

"Yes," he said at last, so low that the word was almost lost on the faint evening breeze. "Yes, John," he said more clearly. "It's worth it. I could never live with myself if I didn't at least make the attempt. I owe it to her. I've come so far now there's no way I could turn back. That would make the last four year a farce, a greater failure than if I try and fail to reach her."

Exasperation was evident as the other man shrugged angrily, half turning away to gaze out over the rolling cemetery fields.

"You owe Evelyn nothing now but a decent respect for her death. I knew her. I loved her almost as much as you did, and I know that it would not please her to see you do this, particularly in her name. You're making her a part of something that…I don't know. It's almost a bizarre carnival. It's futile and self defeating and almost obscene."

It was an old argument, often rehearsed in each of their minds, never with any difference in the outcome. Sheldon was unwilling to rise to the bait. After all, tonight would see the consummation of his endeavors and, one way or another, the end of his quest, his final opportunity to make amends for his neglect.

"John," he said quietly. "There's no reason for you to participate in something that goes so strongly against what you believe. I've told you this before. I have everything that I need. After tonight, I'll listen to whatever you tell me. I'll take that job with your agency that you keep offering and I'll be hard working, down to earth, and relentlessly mundane for the rest of my life. But tonight, just one night, I need a little magic, and I have it here." His eyes shifted to the brass amulet with its hammered metal chain, an unprepossessing charm with a dull surface marred by scarred runes.

Travers dropped his hands to his sides, but they remained clenched with suppressed frustration.

"If there's anything left of your sanity by then." His face wrinkled with self recrimination. "I'm sorry. I know how much this means to you, but I also know how much you mean to me, Paul. You're my oldest friend, the only person I've remained close to over the years, and I can't leave you alone to face the disappointment that I know and you know – somewhere within yourself – is inevitable. I don't like it, but I'll see it through with you. I would never be able to live with myself if I left you here and something happened, something I might have been able to prevent."

Sheldon didn't reply, touched uncomfortably by the emotion in the other man's voice. Both remained silent until the lengthening shadows began to creep upon them from all sides. Finally Travers shook himself out of a prolonged reverie.

"Come on, Paul. We'd better get moving if we're going to go through with this. They'll be driving through soon to shoo out the last visitors, and we don't want to be caught out where they can see us."

His friend nodded in agreement, although he still hesitated to leave the grave site until he felt a hand on his arm. "All right," he breathed. "Let's get out of here."

The two men moved swiftly but without obvious circumspection across the neatly cropped grass, passing through a grove of magnolias in full bloom, their fragile blossoms just reaching the point where they would shower the turf with color. The cemetery was vast, a convoluted expanse of stone and gardens, embellished with literally thousands of flowering shrubs. Although most of the graves were marked with nondescript headstones, one out of five sported a more imposing monument, usually erect slabs of pinnacles, guilty consciences made manifest. Scattered throughout the grounds were perhaps a dozen mausoleums, half buried in the ground so that shrubs grew above, and vines obscured their walls. It was to one of these that the two men hurried.

Earlier that day, Sheldon had contrived to break the lock on this brass bound door, taking care not to damage it so badly that it would not pass casual inspection. Now, in the failing light, the two men shouldered the door open on its poorly lubricated hinges. Stepping inside, Sheldon removed a candle and matches from his pocket while Travers eased the door shut behind them. The lock was necessarily left open and would not fool the cemetery guards if they looked closely, but that eventuality was unlikely. In the dim light provided by the flickering candle, the two men found a stone ledge and sat down to wait.

Time crept slowly by in the damp, musty darkness. Travers smoked a cigarette, then felt embarrassed about disposing of the butt, finally inched the door open and tossed it outside. It was dark enough now that no detectable light entered through the open, but the candle flickered and nearly went out as a sharp, chill breeze disturbed the dust laden air.

"Paul, this is crazy! We're sitting in a crypt, by God! I don't believe it myself and I'm sitting right here waiting with you for midnight so that you can magically recall the spirit of your dead wife and apologize to her for being out of town on a business trip when she died. It's an absurd situation. We're two grown men indulging in a children's fantasy, and you're gambling your sanity on its validity."

Sheldon sighed and leaned back against the wall, his face lined with fatigue, voice thin but still forceful.

"You've involved yourself with this, John; I never asked you to come even though I appreciate your presence, if not your support." When the other man nodded reluctant admission, he went on. "There's far more to it than just my being gone when the accident happened. You know as well as I that I let my work dominate my life to the exclusion of everything else. I spent more than half my nights away and was preoccupied and irritable when I was home."

Travers protested, interrupting him. "She understood that, Paul. She knew that you were at a crucial point in developing your own independent agency. It was a transitional period in your lives."

Sheldon raised his arm as though to cast aside the arguments proposed in his defense. "I overdid it and you know it. If I had wanted a career so much, I should have remained single like you and not have intruded into Evelyn's life. In a way that's immaterial any way; if that was my only cause for guilt I might have been able to live with it. But I became jealous as well. You know that we fought, that I accused her of things that I won't repeat now. There is no way you could realize how frequent, how intense were my baseless suspicions. I recognize that now. I was just working out my frustrations with my customers at her expense. Even at the time I must have known on some level that her clubs and trips and other interests were just ways to fill in the time when I was gone."

He paused for several seconds. "Somehow I won the love of a wonderful woman, and I ignored it, almost destroyed it, finally lost it when she died. I have to ask her pardon or I'll never be able to rest, never knowing whether or not she forgave me for my weaknesses."

"I was with her at the end, Paul. You know that. Her last words were of love, not hate or resentment. You don't have to put yourself through all of this."

Sheldon reached over and patted Travers' leg. "Thank you, John. I really don't doubt your word. But you're a good enough friend that you'd say that even if it weren't true. I appreciate your loyalty, but I must find out from the only unimpeachable source, Evelyn herself."

"And to do that, you're willing to risk your sanity on a piece of mumbo-jumbo?"

"What do I have to lose, John? I have visited the most respected experts on magic in the world, in Haiti, Africa, Ecuador, the

Balkans, San Francisco. In each case, the only hope they could offer was this charm."

He fingered the amulet reflectively. "In conjunction with the proper ritual, this should allow Evelyn's spirit to return to our world for a few moment, a few moments during which she can only speak to the man she truly loves, after which she is lost to the afterworld forever. Even if this is only the mumbo-jumbo that you consider it, I must at least take the chance. It's the only one that I'm likely to ever have."

For a few moments, Travers considered fresh arguments, but at last his shoulders slumped in resignation and he stepped back to wait, smoking another cigarette in the semi-darkness. The crypt had become overtly chilly, a physical as well as psychological weight that pressed down on both men.

Shortly before midnight, the brass door was opened once more and the two men returned to the grave site. Travers held a flashlight now, while his companion sprinkled a circle of dried vegetable matter around the grave, drawing it from a plastic sandwich bag in his pocket. Satisfied finally that the ring was continuous, Sheldon placed the amulet on the center of the grave, then withdrew beyond the circle, ready for the invocation.

He began reciting the short chant in a low voice, gradually working into a rhythmic repetitious singsong. He became oblivious to his surroundings. Travers drew back even further, mildly disturbed by his friend's intensity and wary despite his professed skepticism. The minutes passed, growing closer to the stroke of midnight, the time at which Evelyn's spirit was supposed to manifest itself.

As the critical moment approached, the breeze seemed to quicken and grow cooler, though unaccountably it did not disturb the broken leaves and stems that formed the magic circle. Travers seemed unaffected, oblivious, his concentration centered on the chanted liturgy, the invocation of the dead. And when the change came, Travers wasn't certain whether he was witnessing something tangible, spiritual, or hallucinatory.

A pale translucence began to appear in the air directly above the amulet, apparently issuing forth from within its core. It was a foggy substance that moved independently of the breeze, but with the graceful tentative motions of smoke curling up from the end of a cigarette in still air. As the seconds passed, more of the wispy stuff appeared, increasing its opacity. The chill that Travers felt then was in no way connected to the external temperature and humidity. He blinked his eyes in a futile effort to dispel the vision, his rational nature refusing to accept that his obsessed friend might have actually found a way to bridge the barrier between death and life.

The shimmering figure congealed, becoming almost totally opaque, so that he could just detect the ominous curve of the gravestone barely visible through its substance. It became identifiably human, then feminine, and ultimate resolved into the form of Evelyn Sheldon herself, just as she had looked on the day of her death. Travers blinked his eyes, incredulous, unable to look away.

Sheldon's demeanor had become completely transformed as though he had been rejuvenated by the sight of his dead wife. He took an involuntary step forward, caught himself and stopped. Any penetration of the circle would shatter the materialization. The chant was complete now and he waited for the form of his wife to turn and face him.

Her features were relaxed at first, just as they had been after the morticians had ministered to her. But as she became aware of the two figures standing nearby, her eyes took on the semblance of life, lit from within by a joy of recognition and love that was so evident that neither man at that moment was able to believe that she did not truly live again. She raised her head, spread her arms wide, invitingly, lips moving silently.

Sheldon was momentarily perplexed. Why could he not hear her? The charm was specifically supposed to allow communication, not just this unsatisfactory vision. But she seemed totally mute. Then, from behind Sheldon, Travers spoke softly, just a few short words.

"Yes, Evelyn dearest. I hear you my love."

NOT A GOOD YEAR

The year started off badly and, as you might expect, it got steadily worse. The entire global financial system had been creaking along for some time with its various weak spots patched up with duct tape legislation designed to provide a bridge from one crisis to the next. It was bolstered by progressively more unrealistic wishful thinking, but none of us really believed that it would fail in the long run. The momentum of commerce would carry us through, or so we thought. The government would do something to avert a reckoning. Capitalism was self-corrective and would sustain itself in the fullness of time. We were too sophisticated to really screw everything up beyond redemption. Everything would be fine sooner or later.

There had been growing signs that something was seriously wrong, and even the small book store I managed had been affected. Credit was tighter than ever and I was forced to cut back on acquisitions. When the titles on the shelves stopped changing regularly, I could no longer count on steady income from my usual customers. Since I didn't have the money to increase my advertising, I wasn't luring in any new clientele. My profit declined, which made it even more difficult to purchase new titles. You know the spiral. It's common in the business world and I was at least fortunate in that I really didn't need the income from the store. It was just something to do now that I was retired. Eventually the cycle swings upward and we do better. That probably would have happened in this case as well, but there were other problems that we couldn't have anticipated. Or maybe we could. Some of them anyway.

The news was bad all over, but we'd gotten used to that during the 20th Century. When the world was a much bigger place, we didn't know that a landslide in Afghanistan had wiped out a village, or that flooding in central Africa was causing widespread starvation. A shrinking globe and a sensation happy press rubbed our faces in doom and gloom every day and we became inured to it. And there were other natural disasters much closer to home. Hurricane Bethany outdid Katrina, and no one seriously believed that New Orleans could be rebuilt this time, particularly since the melting ice caps had raised the sea level noticeably. Other coastal areas were nearly as badly hit, although at least they'd had the chance to evacuate in an orderly fashion. The Florida Keys were disappearing and coastlines all over the world were getting an unwelcome facelift. My shop in Providence is high on College Hill so I wasn't worried about flooding, but the expansion of Narragansett Bay still had its impact. The city had lost almost twenty percent of its population in less than a year, which obviously reduced my customer base, and those who were left were too busy salvaging what they could to spend time reading.

It was also getting very expensive to pay for food, thanks to the unprecedented wildfires in California, the drought in the Midwest, and the recent series of devastating earthquakes elsewhere. Fresh produce would have cost as much as fine wine, except that the vineyards were also badly hit and a modest Zinfandel was up to $50 per bottle. There was a farmer's market within walking distance of my house, which was fortunate because gas had increased to $12 per gallon, when it was available at all. Hurricane Bethany and her sister Corinne had wrecked most of our off shore drilling platforms and their cousin Gretchen had severely damaged our refining capacity in Texas. And then there was the corn blight, the mutant cotton weevil, and the tent caterpillar outbreak. Europe and Asia weren't doing much better with the rice paddies underwater and food imports interrupted by strikes, a rise in high seas piracy, and a rash of civil wars and trade embargoes.

Traffic in my store continued to drop. Days would pass sometimes without so much as a browser, and my largest single over the counter sale in May was twenty dollars. On an impulse, I had hired someone to establish a website for my business a couple of years earlier, but I hadn't devoted much attention to it. It was clear now that I needed to expand my presence there if I was going to break even. With the prices of everything else rising almost daily, I wouldn't be able to keep the store open for very much longer if it was operating at a loss. My initial online efforts were promising since the wealthy part of the population had largely retreated into gated communities and did most of their shopping remotely, so I upgraded to a new sales and promotional package. Unfortunately, there were problems with it and I spent a lot of time on the telephone with customer support, based in Mumbai, until a series of tsunamis destroyed much of the west coast of India. Frustrated, I reinstalled the older system that I had abandoned, only to discover that it was incompatible with the latest version of Windows. That meant I had to invest in an alternative system – support based in Belarus this time – which had a lot of bugs but seemed to be working at an acceptable level until the Gotcha Virus appeared.

You remember the Gotcha Virus, I'm sure. It was probably meant to be nothing more than a harmless worm, replicating itself and spreading endlessly, launching popup windows with a smiley face which said "gotcha!" at random moments. Whoever had written the code had come up with a clever idea to deter countermeasures. All of the hidden Gotcha modules kept in continual touch with one another, so if one machine or group of machines was successfully cleaned, its fellows simply restored the problem by making a fresh copy. Most firewalls were unable to recognize the fragmentary segments of code individually and they weren't joined into the active program until they were all in place again. The experts are probably still arguing about what happened next, if there's anyone left to argue. Apparently the immense number of computers affected reached some critical point, and since the code was meant to adapt to efforts to remove it, the basic program altered over time – and not very much time. In combination, the total computing capacity available to all of the separate Gotcha modules surpassed that of the human mind. The prevailing opinion – when it was still possible for there to be a prevailing opinion – was that Gotcha never became truly self aware, but that it functioned as though it was. The fact that PCs, Apples, and Linux based machines were all affected didn't help either.

The world wide web was completely infected. Large portions were shut down in an effort to clean the virus out of the system. The remaining avatars of the Gotcha network struck back in a kind of electronic Armageddon. When it was all over a week or so later, less than one percent of the world's computational capacity had survived, and no one was confident of the integrity of what was left. The banks crashed, international trade reeled, and panic swept the world. Then terrorists exploded nuclear weapons in Volgograd and Orlando. Turkey invaded Iran in response to their support of the Kurds. Israel bombed Syria and moved troops into Lebanon. For no discernible reason, North Korea launched a nuclear strike against Japan. Serbia occupied Kosovo and Russia seized the Crimea. The United States simultaneously launched bacteriological attacks on Cuba and Venezuela. The Russians retaliated by initiating a nuclear strike against both China and the United States, apparently in large part the result of botched communication within the command structure. Both countries responded with what might have been massive counterstrikes. Fortunately the Gotcha virus had spread through the military network as well as the private sector. Only about ten percent of the available missiles were fired, although that was sufficient to inflict widespread destruction. More than one hundred cities died in a single day.

Much of the conflict was brought under control by the end of June, more through mutual exhaustion than as the result of active statesmanship. Although the infrastructure of government and commerce had been weakened everywhere, enough remained that most nations retained their identity, although no one knew much about what was happening in Pakistan, Somalia, Iran, the Pacific Northwest, central Africa, or the interior of South America. Radiation sickness was a major problem and the survivors also had to deal with a wave of varied disease vectors. Plagues were most prevalent in Europe, North Africa, Brazil, and Saudi Arabia but they presented lesser problems virtually worldwide.

The surviving governments, most of which became increasingly autocratic for "the duration of the emergency", tried to keep in touch with one another by radio, but the upsurge in sunspot activity that began in late July disrupted communications so badly that it was difficult even to exert authority over the remotest parts of individual countries. Texas, New Hampshire, and Montana all announced their secession from the United States. I pretty much lost direct knowledge of anything happening outside North America after that, but my sister was a senior officer at the CIA and she kept me relatively well informed. What remained of the American military was by that point engaged in recovering the estimated fifty million unburied dead bodies in the United States, then burning or burying them to discourage the spread of disease. There were no forces available to suppress the widely scattered rebellions. No conventional ones anyway.

But the government was not about to let the three dissident states set an example to be emulated by the other restive regions of the country. It turned out that the Palin administration had secretly financed a wide range of unconventional weapons, including the extensive chemical and bacteriological facility that had developed the targeted plagues used in Cuba and Venezuela. Among their discoveries was a tailored virus which had no affinity for living beings, but which could animate dead tissue. The virus was released systematically in selected areas bordering the three rebellious states and within hours the dead were rising to attack the living. Not the ones already buried, of course. Even if the virus had somehow reached them, they would never have been able to free themselves from their coffins. But there were millions of unburied bodies that had not been laid to rest, many of whom were now called upon to serve their country once again.At first, the program was considered to be an unqualified success. New Hampshire surrendered after three days and Montana followed by the end of the first week. Resistance in Northern Texas crumbled and the Lone Star Army began to retreat while their government frantically tried to open negotiations for a cease fire. That's about the time when a new problem arose.

The counter virus that was supposed to return the dead to their inanimate state proved to be less successful in the field that it had been in the laboratory. Legions of zombies spread into Vermont and northern Massachusetts, and others were seen in Wyoming, Idaho, and New Mexico. The army was forced to take direct action, delaying their cleanup efforts and exacerbating the spread of disease. The military was able to protect major population centers but individual zombies still roamed the countryside and had to be tracked down and disposed of by means of time consuming search operations. A sustained heat wave complicated matters and hastened the putrefaction of both the animate and inanimate dead and a fresh wave of the more familiar plagues – particularly typhus - erupted in August. By the middle of September, the affected areas were pretty much contained but no one knew how many, if any, living people survived in the greater part of nine states. Reconnaissance by air confirmed that there were people moving about, but it was difficult to determine what portion of them had pulses.

The rest of the country was just starting to catch its collective breath about then. The worst of the troubles seemed to be behind us and we were girding our metaphysical loins for the long and difficult task of rebuilding. I wouldn't describe the prevailing atmosphere as optimistic, but the fatalism and despair of the previous season had largely dissipated. Then we heard about the aliens in China.

They'd landed about six weeks earlier, actually. Twenty gigantic spaceships set down one morning along the Chinese border with Mongolia just north of Yinchuan. They had deployed their strike force in several hundred armored vehicles vaguely resembling human tanks, although they were much longer and narrower and were capable of limited, low altitude flight. The aliens used some sort of disintegration ray that interfered with molecular bonding and reduced their targets to dissociated particles. They were also equipped with force shields that repelled almost everything the Chinese military could throw at them. With their usual reluctance to lose face by asking for help, the Chinese had fought the invaders alone and basically in secret until it became obvious that they were powerless to halt the advance. Beijing fell in less than two weeks and the alien forces had paused to regroup, then turned south.

Even if the rest of the countries of the world had been in better shape, it's not clear that we could have done anything to substantially alter the military situation. The aliens – who refused all attempts at communication and who looked disturbingly like Jar Jar Binks on steroids – also generated some sort of field that suppressed nuclear reactions. Not only would atomic weapons not work against them, but every nuclear reactor within range shut down and would not restart. The Chinese had managed to destroy less than a score of their war machines and hadn't even scratched the paint on their ships, still parked in Mongolia. It looked as if the human race was powerless to defeat them and doomed to subjugation, if not extinction.

That's when asteroid 433 Eros hit the Earth. In retrospect, the CIA has advanced the theory that the aliens had been using the near Earth asteroid as a forward observing post and that they had altered its orbit at some point during the previous hectic months without anyone on Earth noticing. This isn't surprising since most of the observatories had been destroyed by then, and those that survived were largely abandoned. Even if they'd been functioning normally, the amount of debris in the atmosphere would have made their normal work impossible. The world has avoided the nuclear winter that had been predicted in the event of a nuclear conflict, but we've been experiencing a very protracted nuclear late autumn.

If the CIA is correct, then apparently the aliens made some sort of miscalculation because the asteroid's new orbit was unstable and it entered the Earth's atmosphere. There is also considerable anecdotal evidence suggesting that the invaders realized their error at the last minute and attempted to destroy 433 Eros before impact, using some kind of beamed weapon that caused it to break up prematurely. This theory is based on stories related by refugees who claimed to have survived the subsequent impact, but there is considerable skepticism about their accounts. Whatever the aliens may or may not have done, it was not effective enough to prevent the shattered fragments from raining down all over northern China, Mongolia and the western Pacific.

The invasion force was virtually wiped out, although there are rumors that small units still remain concealed in ruins. They will no doubt replace the yeti in local mythology.

Although the cataclysm destroyed the invasion force, it was not entirely good fortune for humanity, particularly the millions of Chinese and Mongolians who had survived the alien assault only to have the skies fall. Nor were the effects confined to the impact area. There was another massive disruption of the global weather system. Hurricanes and cyclones were devastating in North America and Europe, particularly the latter where they developed into a superstorm that lashed Scandinavia and the British Isles for more than a week. There were earthquakes on every continent, and serious aftershocks have continued right up through the beginning of December. Volcanic activity has also been widely reported. My sister heard rumors of major eruptions in Hawaii just before the mega-tsunami reduced the islands to bare sand.

Winter came early and has been very bitter. Here in New England we had a blanket of snow on the ground at Halloween that has yet to melt. What remained of heating oil supplies dried up quickly, as did stores of coal and natural gas. Pitched battles have been fought over firewood and local residents have sacrificed most of their flammable materials. I burnt all of my furniture in the fireplace to keep warm and now, alas, I have started carrying home armloads of books to feed the flames. I haven't had a customer in weeks, but then again, I rarely have the energy to open the store. My sister told me that the government is still functioning out of a series of interconnected bunkers, but that efforts to improve the situation in the cities and countryside are on hold until spring, whenever that might come. That was at Thanksgiving. I haven't heard from her since then. The telephone system failed the following week and the postal service is so unreliable that almost no one uses it any more, although I still receive the occasional piece of junk mail.

I was thankful to have survived the year's disastrous events and reassured that at least the situation couldn't possibly get much worse. It will be a difficult winter and a challenging new year, but I remained optimistic that we would, after all, survive and live to rise again. That is, I was optimistic until just recently.

It appears that some idiot named Whately has opened a gateway between universes and invited the Old Ones to return.

Movie Review

Well, readers, I've been to see the newest superhero blockbuster, *The Revengers 2: Age of Precarious*, and it's pretty much what you would expect. First, for all of you non-comic readers, a little background. Although Marvel and DC have dominated the superhero genre for generations, several smaller players have found their own niche. One of the most successful of these is the Cosmic Comics Group, which switched from talking animals to superheroes back in the 1970s.

Their initial offering did not do well. The Scriveners were three famous poets – Byron, Keats, and Shelley – brought back from the dead to fight supervillains and fill dialogue balloons with flowery prose. They only lasted three issues, defeating in order the ghost of Mickey Spillane, the Word Processor, and the POD, and it looked as though Cosmic was going to have to be content with the modest profits from Buzz the Bumblebee and the Jackrabbit Brothers. But fate took a hand when they agreed to honor a pre-existing contract and published the first issue of Captain Atlantis. The main character was a prince of the lost continent who wakened from suspended animation and adopted the United States as his new homeland. Prince Numinous adopted the name Clark Rogers, teamed up with a young American named Lucky Robbins, and defeated several charismatic villains that first year including the Red Skeleton, Dr. Dismal, and the Green Ghoul.

Captain Atlantis was an immediate though limited success and was followed in short order by companion titles including *The Bulk, The Toddler, The Manitou, Centipede Man*, and *The Scarlet Bitch*. There were eventually some crossover stories and in 1980 Captain Atlantis organized the Revengers, which included all of the individual characters except Centipede Man and Doctor Weird. This became the most popular title Cosmic offered, although the individual characters all retained their own magazines with largely independent story lines.

The first Revengers movie appeared in 2010 and did reasonably well but did not generate enough income to pay the salaries of the popular actors who made up the cast. So the second film retained only Captain Atlantis, and he has barely more than a cameo. The death of the Scarlet Bitch, his romantic interest, came in the climactic scene of the first movie, and this provided an excuse for him to temporarily resign from the newly reorganized Revengers at the beginning of the second film. Before he goes he explains the absence of the others. The Bulk lost control of his malleable mass and sank out of sight into the ground, presumed to have been killed when he reached the earth's molten core. The Manitou has been called back to the Happy Hunting Ground by the Great Spirit after being summoned by Doctor Weird – offstage - to defeat the Prestidigitator. The Toddler – who famously bested the Molester in his first outing – is sidelined by the onset of puberty.

Before running off to the Fortress of Solidity to deal with his grief, Atlantis has recruited a new team of Revengers, consisting of the Hummer, Pep Rally, the Condenser, the Androgyne, and the Engineer, all of whom have made appearances – sometimes brief – in the comic books. Since no one is explicitly placed in the leadership role, the Hummer and the Engineer become rivals and their divisiveness is a major subplot.

Their opposition this time is the criminal organization of supervillains known as Medusa, who have recently accepted the Animator as their leader. The Animator has organized a special squad to deal with the Revengers consisting of the Candidate, Ennui, Microaggression, the Dessicator, and the Bodice. The Bodice is the only member never to have appeared in the comics and was probably created to add another woman to the cast to counterbalance Pep Rally.

Since most of the heroes and villains are new to viewers who have not read the comics, the first half of this nearly three hour movie establishes necessarily brief back stories for each. The Hummer has oversized vocal chords and can generate an annoying sound that disrupts the concentration of his foes. Pep Rally is very athletic but her main power is that she improves the mood and enthusiasm of her allies. The Condenser can summon water out of the air through an act of will, the Androgyne can impersonate anyone of either sex, and the Engineer can alter certain physical laws like the coefficient of friction.

On the dark side, the Animator can briefly bring inanimate objects to life, usually statues, photographs, topiaries, and similar things, although in the comics at least he has been known to draw some menacing creature and give it temporary life. The energy must, however, be drawn from another living being. The Candidate is so glib that he can talk his way out of almost any situation, Ennui radiates an aura of doom and gloom that discourages his enemies, Microaggression can utter phrases that physically damage those to whom they are directed, the Dessicator can dehydrate a human body with a single glance, and the Bodice mesmerizes men and women alike by displaying a glimpse of her shapely body, a power she received when her mother accidentally gave her a radioactive training bra.

We learn some of this in flashbacks, some in preliminary clashes between individual characters. The Dessicator dries out the Hummer's mouth and throat so that he is forced to flee for his life. The Androgyne keeps changing gender, race, and other physical attributes so that Microaggression's painful comments misfire, but the fight ends in a draw. Ennui manages to convince the Engineer that some problems are not amenable to a mathematical solution and the latter goes into a fugue state for the entire middle part of the movie.

The good guys are on the ropes until the Hummer convinces them to consult with the Couch Potato, a two thousand pound man who sits in his parents' basement surrounded by television monitors and computer terminals, all attached to his nervous system. He can instantly recall anything that has appeared on any of his input devices, but unfortunately he is completely neutral and not only will he not volunteer information but he will answer questions put to him by the villains as well, which leads to a minor plot complication near the end which I won't spoil for those who haven't seen it yet.

In any case, the Couch Potato has tapped into the communications network of Rick Rage, who is head of a quasi-official government agency known as W.I.E.L.D. (Worldwide Integrated Effort to Limit Damage). Rage has learned that the Animator is planning to replace the entire Supreme Court with animated versions created from their official portraits. Their first target is the most conservative member of the Court, but the plot misfires when Justice Scales proves to be so lacking in humanity himself that his life force will not sustain his animated portrait except in two dimensions, so the plan has to be aborted. By the time they are ready to strike at Chief Justice Waver, the Revengers are ready for them.

This time our heroes have chosen the right matchups, some of which were frankly rather painfully obvious. The Condenser and the Dessicator pretty much cancel each other out, as do the Androgyne and the Bodice, and Pep Rally and Ennui. The Hummer, however, completely defeats the Candidate by disrupting his chain of thought and interfering with the steady force of his rhetoric. The Engineer cleverly nudges natural laws to neutralize the painful content of Microaggression's deadly taunts. The slight advantage held by the Revengers eventually leads to a complete rout, although the Animator shows up and turns the tide by bringing a pride of stone lions to life, along with Smoky the Bear, the Jolly Green Giant, and Mr. Clean. Just when we think all is lost, Captain Atlantis reappears to save the day in a clever trick that I won't reveal here.

Viewers should remember to remain seated throughout the credits. There is a teaser about half way through in which we catch a glimpse of the villain from the next movie. Comics readers will remember that in one memorable story arc, the Revengers traveled to a future in which the NRA took over the world and began inserting human DNA into weaponry, resulting in sentient weapons that eventually seized control of the government. Two of the chief villains from this storyline were Enfilade and the Sniper and their recognizable shapes are seen emerging from a glowing ball of light in a thirty second clip. There is no word yet as to whether any of the cast members of the first movie will return.

Food For Thought

I managed not to flinch when the Tutanken ambassador vomited on the conference table, but I couldn't help wrinkling my nose and averting my eyes. It was obvious that he'd been consuming their customary diet; the foul odor spread through the conference room instantly despite the ventilators. Our own ambassador, Paul Cardigan, had been fitted with a an internal prosthetic regurgitant, and he dutifully leaned forward and spewed a somewhat less unsavory acknowledgment. With the formal greetings concluded, we all pushed back while two almost humanoid robots flushed the formalities into the drains at the four corners of the table. They must have been spraying some form of deodorant into the air at the same time, one probably aesthetically pleasing to the Tutanken, but it was so sweet that my stomach clenched and I might have added my own impromptu salutation if I hadn't carefully avoided eating or drinking anything during the hours immediately preceding this session.

"Greetings. I see you have good eaten." The ambassador prided himself on his ability to speak our language, and protocol as well as decorum prevented us from disabusing him.

Cardigan made no effort to mimic Tutankenese, which sounded like a continuous low rumble to human ears. We had brought a Pulagian translation machine with us and Cardigan spoke slowly and distinctly into what passed for a microphone. The volume was set too high and Nelson, our technician, touched the controls, a bit hesitantly I noticed, but with the desired result.

"It is always a pleasure to merge blessings with such a distinguished host. I see that you also have eaten well." I doubt that Cardigan had examined the exposed contents of Tutuskitor's stomach any more closely than had I, but given the ambassador's stature, it was unlikely that he would have dined on the mundane fare consumed by his staff. "I trust that your larder is amply stocked." The Tutanken were obsessed with foodstuffs, a compulsion which was no doubt linked to their biological past. Back during their prehistory, one of the two moons orbiting Tutan had broken up to form a narrow ring around its primary, causing a disastrous climatic change on the planet that had left the primitive, predatory Tutanken virtually unchallenged at the top of the food chain. Unfortunately, it had also wiped out most of their potential prey. For more than a thousand years, Tutanken stomachs had rumbled with hunger. If they hadn't eventually invented agriculture and animal husbandry, they might never have had the leisure to build a technological culture.

Cardigan and Tutuskitor completed the usual preliminaries, a process which I found soothing in a way, although I tuned out most of the details. My job was to observe rather than listen. The entire session was being recorded and would be analyzed and studied by a small city of linguists, sociologists, xenopsychologists, and other experts. Our experiences with the Pulagi had taught us a difficult lesson. Aliens were alien, more so than we had initially realized. Just as is the case with humans, the words spoken weren't always a direct representation of the message, and since Tutanken body language was by definition alien, negotiations acquired an extra level of density. Somatic clues might be terrifically important. Negotiating with other species had all the complexities of human interaction, but raised to a higher power. My job was to watch for the things cameras and recorders might miss, subtle changes in coloration, posture, even body odor, and throughout each session I conducted a silent monologue, subvocalizing my observations into the recorder embedded in my jaw.

"Have you had leisure to consider the proposal we discussed at our last convening?" Cardigan had moved directly to the trade pact and I snapped back to attentiveness.

Tutuskitor leaned back slightly from the table, which we believed meant that he didn't want to rush into things but was inviting Cardigan to proceed. Cardigan needed to tread carefully, find the right balance between assertion and deference, particularly since the Tutanken were relative newcomers to interstellar travel and were notoriously thin skinned. The ambassador raised both arms above his head and touched his clawed hands together in what would be a perfectly ordinary stretching exercise for a human, but which was probably much more significant. The Tutanken have round, blocky bodies, massing about double that of an average human. They had distinct heads and necks, although you might not immediately realize that this was the case because the head was normally retracted slightly below the shoulders, drawn back into a slight concavity by compression of the rings of cartilage in the neck. The arms, or rather the shoulders, were therefore the highest part of their body; they literally had to reach down to touch the top of their heads. Their faces looked almost human, except that their speaking organ was very small and almost perfectly round. I call it a speaking organ because it wasn't really a mouth. They had two of those, one in each armpit, into which the arms shoveled the smelly and frequently furry food they preferred. I describe his posture and movements in excruciating detail because we believed that the Tutanken supplemented their speech with a much richer language of gesture than do humans. If we were right, Tutuskitor was communicating with his two motionless and silent attendants, telling them something he didn't care to share with the human delegation.

"There is some merit to your proposal, certainly enough to warrant further discussion." That wasn't exactly what he said, but his version of English was so incomprehensible this time that I tuned him out in favor of the translation module in my left ear.

Cardigan almost leaned forward, but caught himself just in time. The Tutanken require a great deal of personal space. "You are satisfied that we can manufacture the items you requested? That we can meet your needs?."

"They meet our minimum specifications, yes, but our present supply arrangements are adequate." From a human, that would be construed as a lie. We knew from the Pulagi and others that Tutanken starships were considered deathtraps even by their own people, that their electronics were so unreliable that one out of ten jumps missed their coordinates, often with disastrous results.

"I am confident that you are correct," Cardigan replied cautiously. "But our studies show that it would be cheaper for you to outsource the components on which we have bid." We had considered pointing out the shortcomings of Tutanken electronics in some tactful fashion, but had decided against it.

"Our mercantile specialists have not contradicted your premise." His eyefolds fluttered, which probably meant that he wasn't comfortable admitting that we were right.

Cardigan pounced. "Was the formal proposal also satisfactory?" A written agreement, painstakingly worded and translated into what we hoped was intelligible Tutankanese, had been sent to Tutuskitor's trade officer two days previously. "We have not been advised of any difficulties with the documents."

Tutuskitor flexed his arms again, almost spastically this time, then dropped them back into the rest position. "You wish to trade for our aqua vitae." I blinked and exchanged a quick glance with Cardigan, whose face betrayed very faint annoyance. One of the Tutanken aides began drumming his fingers against his – or perhaps her – side in what I suspected was the equivalent of my own subvocalizations. They were undoubtedly studying us with just as much interest as we were studying them. Cardigan was piqued because the programmers responsible for the translation device had apparently been tinkering again. We had deliberately chosen to narrowly circumscribe the vocabulary database in the translation equipment. In our previous discussions, the Tutankenese term had been rendered as "medicine". It was important that translations be consistent so that we knew, or at least thought we knew, the subtle differences from one conversation to the next. When they played with the vocabulary storage, it added an unwelcome element of uncertainty to the proceedings.

"It would be most helpful to us, yes." Cardigan's expression was carefully neutral. "As you know, the samples which you provided earlier have proven to be very effective." Indeed they had. The Tutanken might be comparatively backward in physics and engineering but they were pharmaceutical wizards. Shortly after full relations had been established, one of their trade officials had offered the first effective cure for Meta-HIV, which currently afflicted one tenth of the population of Earth. It was unlikely that we could synthesize the drug ourselves for at least several years, and it made sense to trade electronics and other manufactured items during the interim. Cardigan continued through a carefully prepared script, emphasizing that initial shipments would be distributed to and consumed by our most needy cases, but that since a much larger portion of our population could potentially benefit from Tutanken pharmacology, the potential for increased trade was open ended.

Tutuskitor's waist hairs began to move. Actually, they're more like cilia than hair, and we don't really understand their function. But we do know that when they begin to ripple in little waves, it's a sign of distress. The faster the rippling, the greater the degree of upset. The ambassador's waist hair was moving very slowly, but it was definitely in motion. Somehow we'd made a mistake.

"I will consider the matter further, Mr. Cardigan." Tutuskitor was already rising from the bowl shaped seat and Cardigan stood up himself before remembering protocol. Tutanken never raised their eyes higher than those of their hosts. We'd even lowered Cardigan's seat slightly to keep his head slightly below the level of the ambassador. When we met in the human part of the compound, we reciprocated so that we looked slightly down at our guests, but for this session we were in the Tutanken section of the trade complex.

"Shall we discuss it again tomorrow?"

All three aliens were standing now. There was a brief silence before Tutuskitor answered. "If it is convenient for both of us, we shall consider it." And then all three were moving with that odd, rolling gait and they passed out of the room without another word.

The post mortem was mildly ugly. Cardigan knew he'd made an error, but wasn't quite sure what it was, so he took out his frustration on the translator technicians, who insisted that they had done nothing more than refresh the database. He was still angry when he turned to me, but his voice had regained most, but not quite all, of its professional calm.

"Well, Nathan? Any observations you'd like to share with the rest of us?"

"Impressions mostly. Tutuskitor wants to deal with us. We know that the failure rate of their equipment is very high, and that they're currently unable to manufacture to our standards even though they've tried to reverse engineer the samples we've provided. It makes far more sense to trade with us, at least in the short run."

"We know all that," said Vinh, whose department had handled the design of the modules we hoped to sell. "But if he wants to trade, why does he get skittish every time the subject comes up?"

"Something's upsetting him." Chloe Kundalana, staff xenobiologist, looked up from the screen where she'd been reviewing the recordings of that morning's session. "He exhibited mild distress when you expressed interest in their drugs, but calmed down almost immediately. But a moment later, he was moderately disturbed, enough so that he cut the meeting short."

I'd missed the first falter. "Can you suggest a trigger?"

She shook her head. "It could be anything. Maybe one of you inadvertently made an obscene gesture?" We had all been trained to keep our bodies, particularly our arms, as motionless as possible to avoid sending any unintended messages.

"You're looking at the replay, Chloe." Cardigan's voice hardened. "You tell us."

There was a brief, awkward pause while she ran the recording back and forth. "No, nothing, unless it's so subtle I can't detect it."

"Then it has to be something we said, something mistranslated or misinterpreted. Whatever it is, we need to find it, ladies and gentlemen."

But we didn't. Two hours later, we still hadn't a clue. The first, minor upset had come when Cardigan suggested that trade would help meet the needs of the Tutanken. It was possible that Tutuskitor had been mildly insulted, interpreting our position as a suggestion that his people's industrial abilities were somehow inferior. But Chen Lo, Chief Xenopsychologist, disagreed. "There's no evidence of racial chauvinism of that sort among the Tutanken. They're perfectly willing to admit to having shortcomings. After all, they're the ones who told us about the high failure rate of their electronics."

"Perhaps it's an idiosyncrasy of Tutuskitor himself rather than a racial trait," suggested Cardigan. That set off another round of arguments from the subset of people who were trying to profile the ambassador as an individual rather than as a type.

The second and more noticeable reaction came when Cardigan said: "Initially what you provide will be rationed to those with the most pressing need."

"Perhaps he thought that we were being critical because they couldn't synthesize the drugs more quickly," someone suggested. "He might have assumed we were blaming them for the continued suffering of people who had to wait for the treatment."

"That doesn't fit with their profile," responded Dr. Feyd. "They're very much like us in that regard. I think Tutuskitor genuinely feels empathy for our situation, but he wouldn't feel guilty just because he can't cure all our problems at the drop of a hat."

"Are we sure of that?" It was someone I didn't recognize; the makeup of the contact group changed almost weekly. "Could he be lying to us?"

Feyd dismissed this with a head shake. "These aren't Pulagi. Everything we've seen to date indicates that they say what they mean and mean what they say. They don't resort to subterfuge or posturing. It's what they don't say that's the problem. The longest meeting we've had with them was less than thirty minutes, and it takes at least a quarter hour to get past the unpleasant opening formalities."

That set off an argument about the possibility of a racial attention deficit disorder that I'd heard several times before. The level of rancor rose and I shook my head wearily and glanced at Cardigan. He apparently shared my feeling that we weren't accomplishing anything because he adjourned us a few minutes later.

"But I expect to have reports from every section first thing tomorrow morning. I want this solved quickly, folks. If I have to empty my stomach too often I'm going to empty a few offices as well."

I started to leave, but Cardigan caught my eye. "Just a minute, Shaver. I want to talk to you."

We waited until everyone else had filed out of the room, some subdued, some defiant, most just puzzled or worn out or both. The Tutanken seemed, despite their physical differences, much closer to humans psychologically than any of the other races we'd encountered so far. That just made it more frustrating when things went badly.

"I'm thinking about sweetening the offer."

"I don't understand."

"Maybe this is just a negotiating ploy to make us reduce the price."

I shook my head. "We vetted this with the Pulagi, remember? They told us our terms of exchange were fair, even slightly favoring the Tutanken."

"I know that, but the Pulagi are capable of making mistakes just as much as we are. Do you have any idea how many people die of Meta-HIV every day, Shaver? We're talking about saving people's lives."

"And our electronics would save Tutanken lives. They've sent twelve ships to Earth so far and only ten of them arrived safely. They need our equipment just as much as we need their serum."

"So why won't they negotiate?"

"I don't know." I shook my head. "We're missing something, something in their racial psychology. I don't think this is a bargaining ploy, Mr. Ambassador. I don't think cost has anything to do with it."

"We need an answer, Nathan. And quickly."

I felt the weight of the problem land squarely on my shoulders. That shouldn't have been the case. I was part of a team, a very large team, and my talent was for observation, not analysis. It wasn't fair or reasonable to expect me to come up with some miraculous answer just because I'd once had a moment of insight that had gotten us past a crisis with the Pulagi. Someone else needed to step up to the plate this time, because I was just as mystified as everyone else.

But it doesn't work that way. People raise their expectations of you when you've made a big score. I was even a little disappointed with myself, as though I'd let the team down by not coming up with an immediate answer. Rationally I knew I was being unreasonable, but reason doesn't have a lot to do with feelings.

So I went back to the closet that I called an office and thought about it some more. Then I reviewed the recordings of all previous meetings between humans and Tutanken in which our visitors had shown physical evidence of alarm or discomfort. The side scrolling window on my screen provided commentary which I also read. In every case, the reaction had subsequently been explained. Either humans had encroached on the individual's personal space, or there had been a mistranslation, or one of the humans had stood up prematurely while functioning as guest, or there was some other discernible explanation.

With one exception.

The first Tutanken expedition had entered our system unannounced and caused considerable alarm until the Pulagi embassy identified the newcomers and reassured the world government about their intentions. Things had progressed slowly but systematically after that, although there was still a significant portion of the public who distrusted the reclusive nature of the Tutanken. Their first contact team had been more outgoing, had even requested and received permission to have guided tours of human cities and institutions. They were particularly interested in our agricultural and food distribution systems, which made even more sense after we'd learned about their racial history.

Despite their ungainly appearance, they were physically a lot closer to humanity than any other species we'd met. They could breathe our air without augmentation, though it smelled bad to them just as theirs did to us. More significantly, humans and Tutanken could eat each other's food, or some of it anyway, without becoming sick, although in neither case did it provide much nourishment. A human diplomat who had hosted one of the first Tutanken visitors, a female named Velvator, had decided to treat his guest to something special and brought her to one of the finest restaurants in New Manhattan.

Fortunately, we'd learned enough about their physiology by then that one of the diplomat's aides was able to correctly interpret the visitor's distress. Her waist hair had begun rippling wildly and the tympani on the sides of her head had darkened. Although Velvator had recovered as soon as they were outside, she'd asked to be returned to her quarters, and none of the Tutanken had accepted invitations for private tours since that day.

The event had triggered a massive study effort that still hadn't adequately explained the event. Clearly the upset had something to do with the consumption of food, which was a known Tutanken preoccupation, and the only subject about which their remarks were often oblique. At times it seemed that they thought of food and eating the same way we thought about feces and elimination, distasteful necessities. But their trade mission ate together publicly in a fully equipped communal kitchen, and never demonstrated any reluctance to allow humans to see them in the act of consuming food. In fact, their communal dining hall was the only room in their embassy with transparent walls, and it was prominently situated near the main entrance so that every visitor had a clear view of its interior.

When I finally gave up and went home, the sun had long since vanished from the sky.

Tutuskitor agreed to another meeting the following day. The verbal formalities were truncated this time; the ambassador apparently wanted to move directly to the details of the trade pact, and Cardigan quickly responded in kind. The Tutanken counter offer was detailed, complex, and comprehensive. They were asking for some concessions in delivery times and offering slightly more favorable terms in exchange. They also wanted the right to negotiate directly with private companies in the future rather than through the government, and offered to allow humans to visit their world for similar purposes. It was a lot more than we expected, and to my admittedly unsophisticated sensibilities in these matters, it sounded like a very good offer.

If I was reading Cardigan's body language correctly, so did he, but he was too much the diplomat to give away the game. He was silent for a few seconds after Tutuskitor finished, or rather, after the translation machine was done, then spoke slowly and carefully. "That's a very interesting proposal, Mr. Ambassador. I will need to confer with my superiors, of course, but I'm optimistic about the results. Your offer includes a great deal to digest, however. Perhaps we could adjourn until the same time tomorrow?"

My head started to ache when I noticed that Tutuskitor's waist hairs were swirling. Cardigan's remarks had been so innocuous. What could possibly have caused such pronounced agitation?

"My duties may prevent that." I had to rely on the translator completely this time; Tutuskitor had abruptly switched to his own language. "I shall need to confer with my own superiors as well. It may be that I have through error exceeded my own authority."

Cardigan glanced in my direction, clearly alarmed, but I couldn't offer him even a gesture of reassurance. Tutuskitor was on his feet and out the door within seconds, his two attendants close behind.

The meeting that followed was highly unpleasant, and my headache quickly went from mild discomfort to pounding throb. I think much of Cardigan's anger was because he was the face of our team; he had been the physical instrumentality of whatever mistake we had made, even though we had all been involved in formulating strategy. He shouted at people and some of them shouted back. Others sat silently, disconsolate, and that was even worse. When we finally broke up, there was an air of doom and gloom that hung over each of us like a shroud.

I went back to my office and stared at the wall for a while. A long while. At some point Nellie, the office secretary, brought a sandwich, a plate of fries, and a cup of coffee, left them on my desk without a word. I ignored the food for a while, but eventually my stomach started to grumble. I hadn't eaten all day; I never ate when we were scheduled to meet with the Tutanken, for obvious reasons. The fries were cold by then but I nibbled at them anyway.

I had finished the sandwich and most of the fries before my stomach stopped rumbling. Fried food always disagreed with me, so I'd probably be up all night with diarrhea or indigestion or both. And then I thought about that some more, and a little light started to go on somewhere in the murky interior of my mind.

Still holding a limp fry in my hand, I left the office and walked down to the translation station.

Anita Koos was the only one there. She was sitting at her desk, staring at a monitor that was split into two windows, apparently comparing text from one side against the other. She looked up as I came in, her eyes following the fry that I brandished like a baton.

"Anita, tell me again how the translator works."

She raised her eyebrows. "Mechanically, logically, or functionally?"

"Word choice. How does it decide which word to use?"

"Well, we have tables of matched vocabulary. There's a master routine that looks for idiomatic expressions and translates them as a unit, of course, but most of the time it's a simple lookup. The Tutanken grammatical system is actually much simpler than our own. They don't have compound sentences or nested dependent clauses."

"But how does the translator choose from similar terms? Why would it pick 'door' over 'entrance', for example?"

"Like I said, a lookup table. With human languages, we'd be a little more sophisticated, because the two words you just suggested aren't always synonymous. But with other races, we collapse the language to as few terms as possible to avoid ambiguity. The results can be a bit awkward at times, and probably make us sound like the village idiot, but they minimize the chance of a translation error."

"How exactly do you collapse it?"

She sighed. "Okay, here's the layman's version. We have a complete human vocabulary on line. We reorganize all the words into groups. One of those groups would include 'door' and 'entrance' and 'accessway' and 'entry point' and probably a lot of others I can't think of. We call this group 'door'. The group 'door' is then matched to a single word in the alien vocabulary, which is also the name given to an actual group of synonyms."

"So whichever of the words we use, the translation machine will render it as 'door'?"

"Yes, and translate it as the group word in the alien language. Is this leading someplace?"

"I think so. Can I get a copy of the vocabulary tables?"

"Not a print out. It would fill a room. It's on line though. I can give you read only access if you want."

"Please."

Three hours later I called Paul Cardigan and got him out of bed. An hour after that we were sitting in his office with Anita Koos and Lars Ragland, the head of Protocol. All three looked irritable and sleepy, but I didn't care.

"I think I know what's wrong."

Cardigan nodded at me. "So you said. Enlighten us."

"The problem is in the translation." Anita started to protest but I waved her down. "Please, hear me out. It's not your fault. It's no one's fault, really. We just underestimated the Tutanken obsession with food. You're all familiar with the Velvator incident?"

Three heads nodded. "What has that got to do with the trade negotiations?" Ragland sounded almost belligerent.

"I think I understand part of the reason what went wrong then, and there's a parallel to our current problem. We know the Tutanken have no taboo against eating in public, right?" Three nods, two of them reluctant. "So what's the difference between a human restaurant and a Tutanken communal eating area?" They exchanged looks but no one suggested an answer. "Waiters." I sat back in my chair and crossed my arms.

"Waiters?" Ragland looked back and forth between the other two. "You think they have a taboo against waiters?"

Cardigan leaned forward, his voice level. I could tell that he was restless, but that he desperately wanted an answer. "Nathan, can you be a little less cryptic? It's been a long and frustrating day."

"All right, here it is. I think our visitors have a phobia about the preparation or maybe just the transfer of food from one adult to another. I went through some recordings we made in their embassy and in every instance the Tutanken prepared their own food and ate separately. They all use the same dining area, but if you watch them, the act of eating is always a profoundly individual act. In the few cases where crowding forces two or more to share a table, they sit as far from one another as possible and take great care never to come near each other's food."

Ragland nodded grudgingly. "It's an interesting observation, certainly worth pursuing. But I don't see what relevance it has to the negotiations. We haven't suggested a dinner party."

"Well, actually, in a manner of speaking we have."

There was some restless stirring at this point and I let it die down, enjoying a bit of sadistic glee at their confused discomfiture.

"There were three occasions during which Tutuskitor became disturbed during our last two meetings. The first was when Paul suggested that they might want to suggest some language of their own in the trade agreement."

Cardigan nodded. "But why would that upset them? They did in fact have a detailed counterproposal."

"He was upset because that's what you said, but that's not what he heard. Your exact words were 'send us some provisions of your own'. 'Provisions', according to the vocabulary tables, is a synonym for 'food', so what you actually did was ask them to send us some of their food."

I paused to let that sink in. Paul picked up on it right away, as did Anita. It took Ragland a little longer.

"Later that same day, you told him that the drugs would be 'rations for the most immediately needy', which I suspect was rendered as 'food for the hungriest' or something very close. He must have known that you didn't mean that literally, but it still must have sounded like an obscenity."

"Oh my God!" Anita covered her mouth with one hand and sat back in her chair. Ragland looked puzzled, but thoughtful. Paul was being inscrutable.

"The meeting today was the worst of all. You told Tutuskitor that the trade agreement would be 'a lot to digest'. Again, I don't think he literally thought you were talking about eating their trade goods, but the very hint of it was enough to trigger their racial phobia. The Tutanken were half starved for scores of generations; they survived by providing for their families and never sharing food with anyone else. The ritual vomiting to open meetings is to demonstrate that both parties have been well fed and therefore don't covet each other's larders. I wouldn't be surprised if their terms for eating and food aren't obscenities, that they talk around the subjects among themselves without ever being too explicit about it. If I'm right, at best we've been making crude comments; at worst, we've been suggesting that they join with us in obscene acts."

There was a prolonged silence before Paul nodded and started to relax. "Okay, so how do we fix it?"

"First we fix the vocabulary tables." I glanced at Anita, who nodded enthusiastically. "And then we have to convince Tutuskitor that we aren't trying to steal his groceries."

Everything went well after that, with Cardigan reading from a freshly prepared script and choosing his responses very carefully whenever he had to extemporize. The first mass shipment of the Mega-HIV cure arrived right on schedule, in a Tutanken ship operating with human constructed jump components.

I amused myself for a while playing with the collapsed vocabulary tables, devising scenarios similar to the ones we'd actually experienced. In doing so I stumbled across one that could have been catastrophic. The serum was not the only Tutankanese item in which we were interested. There were perfumes and some shimmering synthetic fabrics and various other items which looked very pormising. In an early draft of one of Cardigan's presentations, fortunately for a side agreement that we'd decided to defer, he planned to tell Tutuskitor that human consumers would welcome his people with open arms. Considering where the Tutanken keep their mouths, this would have been a particularly unhappy choice of words.

Now there's food for thought.

Parties of the Two Parts

Nathan Shaver watched with interest as two Choktri performed an elaborate ritual in the courtyard below his window, wondering idly how long it would be before one of them pulled off an arm to indicate its interest in mating. There might be advantages to having a modular body but it was frequently disconcerting to those who didn't.

"What's going on, Nathan?" Terry Watson came to the window and put a hand on his shoulder. She looked out before he could answer and he could feel her fingers tighten almost painfully. "Damn! Why do they have to do that inside the compound?"

"It's a biological imperative with them."

"It's obscene is what it is." She crossed her arms tightly in front of her and shuddered.

Nathan knew that Terry had been with the first contact team, and that she'd watched a close friend die when one of the Choktri pulled Frank Leslie's arm out of its socket. It had been meant as a friendly gesture, of course. The Choktri had virtually no contact outside their own culture and this particular individual hadn't realized that human limbs weren't detachable.

The pair in the courtyard must have reached some understanding because both removed their left arms simultaneously. The exchange went smoothly and the arms locked into the shoulder sockets of what were now a mated pair. They had both been rendered asymmetrical, of course, because the taller one was heavier as well. Over time, what passed for DNA in silicon based life would find a compromise and each of the twosome would gradually encompass traits from the other.

"Young love," he sighed dramatically. "Kind of gets to you, doesn't it?" He turned and playfully punched his companion's shoulder.

"You are one sick cookie," said Terry, shaking her head.

"Just trying to empathize with the local culture." His tone was light, but his thoughts were darker. The mating ritual didn't disturb him; he knew that there was minimal discomfort involved. But how did you establish meaningful communication with a species among whom the concepts of individuality and selfhood were so malleable? Swapping arms wasn't a big deal in itself. A human with a prosthetic limb was still the same person. But Choktri memories were distributed throughout their nervous system. Each half of the pair would initially retain its original personality, but during the first few local days after the exchange, both would be altered by the new memories, experiences, and predispositions of their partner. They would be transformed by the process and, according to Choktri law, each was thenceforward a new entity. The pair in the courtyard could disavow all of their past obligations – debts, promises, contracts, even crimes. So how did one negotiate a mutual defense treaty, or any other legal instrument, when the opposite side could effectively abrogate the agreement by simply trading body parts with a neighbor?

"Any progress with the negotiations?"

Nathan shrugged. "What negotiations? We'd made some progress with Tershib but then Tershib met Wilpat and now we don't know whether to continue with Terpat or switch our attention to Wilshib."

Terry rolled her eyes. "I thought Tershib had been thoroughly vetted."

"We all thought that. We studied all of the Choktri officals, or what passes for officials here, and when Tergil and Fayshib exchanged limbs, we figured Tershib would be stable for the foreseeable future so that's where we focused our efforts."

"Barely past the honeymoon and already lusting after another appendage, I gather."

"It's unusual, at least we think it's unusual, for a newly bonded individual to transform again so quickly, but that's what happened."

"You don't suppose it was intentional, do you? If you maneuvered Tershib into a position where he thought he was at a disadvantage, maybe he transformed deliberately to reset the game to the first play."

Nathan ran one hand through his hair and glanced back down toward the courtyard. The newly bonded pair had walked off together. "The thought had occurred to me. But I'm damned if I can think of any way we could have done anything about it even if we'd realized what would happen."

"It's a little easier dealing with their commercial entities, but not much. The Gupta Guild signed off on our initial proposals and they're bound by the protocol under their law even if they all toss their heads in a bucket and pick them out at random. But it's frustrating trying to clear up misunderstandings when the person you negotiated with is now partly the person who opposed the negotiations in the first place." She sighed. "We don't even have the right vocabulary to describe the situation here."

Nathan envied her on that score. The Choktri had solved the problem of internal stability by creating artifices which remained immutable, at least until their charters expired. One could negotiate a binding agreement with one of these artifices and expect minimal duplicity. They used these legal entities for social, trade related, and governmental purposes, although the last was not as clear cut. Although there were no nations among the Choktri, they had as many different governments as did humans. There was a separate government – humans would call them agencies – for every regulated aspect of life on the planet, but there was no single central authority that oversaw the individual organizations. When their interests overlapped, they negotiated settlements. Even worse, from a human point of view, was the ephemeral nature of these artifices. Whenever a term expired, every ruling, procedure, and policy of that entity became null and void unless adopted by the succeeding authority.

Nathan was engaged with the Artifice for External Affairs, administered by twelve Choktri who, until recently, had followed the lead of the progressive Tershib, who had seemed amenable to the establishment of a human refueling and transfer station in the Choktar system. Then the Choktri version of romance had intervened and it was not clear whether Terpat, who seemed to have retained a mostly favorable predisposition toward the treaty, or Wilshib, who was even more isolationist than his lineal antecessor, Wilpat, would prove to be dominant.

Peri Ravanthani made that point again during the morning briefing. The talks had stalled and the briefings served more as a mantra than anything else. This was Ravanthani's first assignment as lead negotiator and he felt trapped in a winless situation that would doom his career unless he could find a scapegoat. As number two in the chain of command, Nathan was acutely aware that he was the candidate of choice for that honor. Sometimes he thought humans were even more devious than the Choktri, and with less excuse.

"Assuming that we manage to find a way around the present impasse," Ravanthani's tone implied that this was a self inflicted wound and that he was trying to decide who was responsible, "we still have the long term problem of transition. Anything new on that front, Nathan?"

"We've explored the possibility of a permanent grant of rights, but it doesn't appear feasible. When the current membership's term expires in two years, all of their decisions become null and void."

Ravanthani sighed. "So even if we came to terms, we would have to start all over again in two years, and every ten years thereafter. I still don't understand that. How can they function if every law has to be passed again after each election?" The Choktri didn't actually have elections. No one fully understood the Directed Consensus process except the Choktri, if even they did.

"Each artifice can establish temporary measures to carry them over the gaps. But these all have a stated expiration date that varies considerably. They provide a kind of bridge between administrations."

"We can hardly ask our superiors to invest in building a significant installation that might have to be dismantled a few years later." Ravanthani made it sound like an accusation. "You're saying this is an exercise in futility, that even if we reach an agreement on terms, it could be abrogated long before the investment would have paid for itself."

Shaver held his peace. He'd been in this game too long to respond to the gambit. But as soon as the session broke up, he walked down to the research section and knocked on Connie Layton's door. "What brings you down here among the peons so bright and early, Nathan?" She settled behind her desk.

"I need some insight into Choktri social customs."

"You've read my briefings?"

He nodded. "Impeccably organized and written and no doubt entirely accurate. Also quite superficial and fairly useless in the present situation."

Connie raised her hands dismissively. "We've only been on site a short time and we're dealing with a silicon based intelligent race with a civilization twice as old as ours."

"I'm not trying to minimize the difficulties."

"But you want a shortcut."

"Precisely."

She sat back in her chair. "Science doesn't work that way you know. My colleagues would disapprove."

"I'm not asking your colleagues. I'm asking you." He felt mildly awkward presuming on their long and at one time intimate friendship, but only mildly.

"If I thought I knew a way to make the negotiations easier, I'd tell you, Nathan. But I don't."

He nodded. "I realize that, but if the Choktri are immortal, they won't think twice about stalling for years, centuries even. We don't have that long."

Connie shook her head. "They're not properly speaking immortal. I was very specific there. The Choktri are potentially immortal because an individual's actual memories are passed along physically with the transfer of body parts. Theoretically, every memory of every individual since they became sentient could have survived to the present, though they'd be dispersed across the entire race. In practice, there has been considerable loss. The Choktri are rugged by our standards but they do die in accidents and natural disasters and there are even occasional murders. And some data is lost because of physiological problems."

"How do they manage to deal with tens of thousands of years of memory?"

"They don't. Most of it is essentially in offline storage. They can retrieve those memories but it takes a conscious effort. We don't really understand the process. In that sense they're a lot like humans. What did you have for breakfast on your tenth birthday?"

Nathan blinked. "I have no idea."

"Neither would a Choktri. But he could ferret that memory out if necessary. "

"All right, but if that's the case, if all the memories of their race have been preserved and dispersed, why aren't they more homogeneous? Their personalities vary as much as ours."

"You're assuming we're simply products of our experiences."

"Isn't that what you said about the Choktri?"

"Ah, you do read my reports. If I remember correctly, however, I said that I was oversimplifying. And they're really not that different from us if you think about it. Let's say that on Earth there are only one hundred possible human experiences and that within a human lifetime an individual could only process ten of those."

Nathan nodded. "Go on."

"There would come to nearly one hundred trillion possible combinations, or personalities, possible. Now imagine that we're talking one hundred trillion possible experiences and a capacity of even one million per person."

"All right, I see your point. So when two Choktri mate, the original individuals effectively die and new ones are created."

Connie shook her head. "No, not really. Are you the same person now that you were when you were eighteen?"

"God, no. I was self centered and convinced that I knew all the answers."

She smirked. "You haven't changed all that much. But the young Nathan Shaver didn't die. He just assimilated new experiences and adapted. With the Choktri, those changes come in concentrated doses when they mate. With us, they accumulate gradually. The end result is pretty much the same."

She stood up abruptly. "Let's take a walk."

They left the offworld compound and walked across the open landscape to the nearest city entrance, painted red so that it stood out from the uniform yellow of the brickwork construction. Choktri technically didn't have cities any more than they had nations. They lived in vast warrens so large that they were readily visible from orbit, but the individual warrens had no distinct institutions or rules of governance. They had reached general consensus on all of the important issues eons earlier and if something should change in the future, it would change for everyone.

Nathan had been inside the city many times, but always as part of the negotiating team and there had been little time for sightseeing. Connie and the other scientists had taken advantage of the remarkable openness of the Choktri and roamed the streets unhindered, although there was a carefully written code of conduct designed to avoid any behavior remotely offensive to their hosts.

There was no pattern to the streets – tunnels actually – and Nathan was lost almost immediately. Connie assured him that she knew the route and could in any case read the inscriptions cut into the walls. They passed a steady flow of Choktri going about their own business, not one of whom gave the humans a second look.

Eventually the modular rooms grew larger and they passed through a market of some sort, then an amphitheater where a small audience watched a group of ten or twelve colorfully caparisoned performers move about the stage in an intricate pattern. "It's roughly analogous to ballet, but without music," Connie explained. "Ideally no pattern should ever be completely duplicated during a performance. We think it's a statement of their racial philosophy, that no personality should ever be replicated."

They moved on. Nathan was about to ask where they were going when Connie slowed the pace and turned into a branch tunnel. "It's just ahead."

The tunnel ended at an indoor park, or at least that's what Nathan thought at first. The chamber was open to the sky and the grounds were covered with the local equivalent of grass and a few taller plants, various forms of the spiky flora of Choktar. At first he thought the area was deserted but then he saw the smallest Choktri he had ever seen, and then another even smaller.

"Is this some kind of nursery?"

Connie nodded. "Yes. It services the entire warren."

Nathan glanced around. "It's not very big."

"Doesn't have to be. There are a half million residents in this warren and only about a dozen children. Budding is a very time consuming and totally voluntary process, which is why their population is so stable."

"So how does that work? Are the kids, the buds, copies of their parent?"

Connie shook her head. "No, it doesn't work that way. There's no actual replication of experience. The information passed on to the new individual is minimal and is completely lost to the parent."

Nathan frowned. "Wouldn't that mean that the child has to learn everything from scratch? Even how to eat and speak?"

"No, they start off fully functional. How many meals have you eaten in your life?"

Nathan shrugged. "Tens of thousands."

"Then it wouldn't bother you to lose the memories of a few hundred, would it?"

"I get it. And I've had thousands of conversations as well. Okay, I see how it works, sort of. But how does the parent decide which memories to pass along?"

It was Connie's turn to shrug. "It's not a conscious process, so far as we know. Maybe the Choktri store memories by type and pass on a few of each category when they bud. We just don't know."

"Couldn't you ask them?"

She shook her head. "We've tried. Their physical sciences, mathematics, and astronomy are all very advanced, but by our standards their biology is pretty primitive. Since they don't get sick, they've never had a strong incentive to develop sophisticated medical knowledge. They were astonished when we told them that human children had to spend years learning to survive on their own. The ones you see here will leave as soon as they've grown enough mass to allow them to mate with a mature Choktri and absorb a wider knowledge base. It takes a couple of years, but they're a patient race."

"It all feels like a closed system. The Choktri are like machines assembled from an array of experiences, actual and transferred."

"Essentially so are we. Our personalities are shaped by what happens to us, and what we read or learn at second hand."

"But we have free will. We make choices that determine what those experiences will be. The Choktri have to accept the consequences of every mating."

"But they're free to choose their mates, and more importantly, they decide what to transfer into their offline storage and what to retain in their working memory. Tershib was much more in favor of our proposal than Wilpat, right?"

"Yes."

"Well, if it was simply an autonomic biological process when they mated, Terpat should have been slightly less inclined to favor us and Wilshib slightly more so."

He thought about it. "Sounds right."

"But while Terpat has indeed become less enthusiastic, Wilshib is actually more opposed than ever. One chose to moderate its opinion, but the other didn't. It's not preordained; they have free will. Or at least as much as we do. They just exercise it slightly differently."

Back at the compound, Nathan tracked down Brian Takahami, the head of the xenocultural team. Brian was looking harried – he always looked harried – but he grudgingly agreed to share a lunch and whatever insights he could provide.

"So tell me what precisely you want to know so that I can explain why I have no way of answering your question." They were sitting in the makeshift cafeteria, pretending that the food in front of them was edible.

"Tell me how the Choktri handle real estate, property rights."

The other man smiled. "I can actually answer that one. They don't. The closest they come to what we think of as property ownership might be called squatter's rights. If Choktri Gabrat is currently living at 111 Tralala Tunnel, then no other Choktri would even consider trying to move in without an invitation."

"But suppose Gabrat mates with Labfest. Who gets the apartment, Gabfest or Labrat?"

"That's up to the two successor identities. They preserve their presumptive rights to their predecessor's abodes. In some rare cases, they share a domicile afterward, but that's very unusual."

"How do they handle population growth then?"

Brian frowned at a spoonful of stew as though trying to identify the constituents, then apparently thought better of it and gulped it down. "The population is incredibly stable. Their rate of reproduction is only slightly higher than the attrition rate. When necessary they extend the warren to accommodate new housing."

"So how did the Droogee acquire rights to build the offworld compound?" The Droogee had been the first race to contact the Choktri, five hundred years earlier.

"We don't know the whole story, but it's significant that there is no physical connection between the compound and the warren. The Choktri gave them permission to create this place as a temporary facility, and since every extension of a warren is meant to be permanent, there had to be space between them. Apparently the Droogee tried to negotiate a long term solution, but gave up after a couple of centuries. Even the Droogee have limits to their patience."

"But the Droogee have been gone for almost two hundred years and we were told that the compound was at our disposal. Doesn't that imply some sort of assignment of rights?"

Brian shrugged. "Maybe they just had no use for it. Maybe since it isn't physically connected to a warren, it is available to whoever chooses to claim it."

Nathan shook his head. "If that was the case, we could just build our transfer station orbiting the next planet out. But they've refused to agree to any permanent facility within their system."

"I can't help you there?" Brian raised his fork, displaying a brownish mass. "What do you suppose this is?'

That evening, he and Connie Layton went for a walk around the perimeter of the Choktri warren. It was a pleasant day and if it hadn't been for the slightly metallic smell of the air, they might have been in some mildly arid part of the Earth. Their walk was uneventful and solitary; Choktri rarely ventured from their warrens. But they did encounter one lone chunky figure who was painstakingly arranging three of the distinctive yellow warren bricks in a pyramid.

"What do you suppose this one's up to?" asked Nathan. Without a translation machine, they could not possibly converse with a Choktri.

"Actually, I know what he's doing. The warren is being expanded here and he's currently assigned to the construction team."

"Not much of a team." Nathan looked around. The area was deserted and there was no sign of any construction underway except for two or three other pyramids, one of them four bricks high.

"They take turns. This is its shift."

"You're pulling my leg. At this rate it would take years to add one living area."

"Decades probably. The Choktri plan ahead."

"I suppose if you're virtually immortal, you can afford to. They probably think we're peculiar because we're always in so much of a rush."

"I wouldn't be surprised. Why are you, Nathan? In such a rush, I mean."

He shrugged. "I'm a product of my profession. In the diplomatic corps, if you're not actively moving up the ladder, then your career is effectively over."

"So what happens if the negotiations here fail?"

"I'll probably be reassigned as an analyst compiling reports that no one reads. And with my luck, Peri Ravanthani will be one desk away from me doing the same." He glanced back at the Choktri. "But I suppose then I'll have time to build a mansion for myself, one brick at a time." He glanced at his chrono. "Time to start back.

We're going to try again today. Peri thinks he might make some headway if he suggests that we might move to another system."

"It won't work."

"I know."

Nathan experienced a profound sense of déjà vu during the next few hours. He could often predict what Wilshib or Terpat was going to say well before the translation software presented a response in an approximation of human language. But eventually he realized that something had changed. At first he thought that the Choktri had adopted some subtly different strategy, but the difference was actually in his perception, or rather, in his interpretation of what he was perceiving.

The Choktri were not stalling, he decided. They were waiting for the human negotiators to do something. But what? Over the course of months, Ravanthani had presented a broad menu of forms of compensation, an outright grant of credit, technological advisers, most favored planet status, a defensive treaty, and had even invited the Choktri to propose terms of their own. The Choktri had discussed each possibility interminably and seemed to enjoy concocting new combinations for what almost seemed aesthetic rather than practical reasons. Nathan was reminded of the pseudo-ballet Connie Layton had shown him.

But no combination had pleased all of the Choktri negotiators and unanimity was required before things could go forward. Were the Choktri deliberately stonewalling? It made no sense. Whatever the final terms, the Choktri would be big winners. It was almost as though they were waiting for the humans to provide some new initiative.

And then, just as Ravanthani was slumping back into his seat, obviously frustrated, Nathan experienced an epiphany.

He leaned toward his superior. "Can I try something?"

Ravanthani looked as though he was in pain. "Why not? Things couldn't get any worse."

Nathan ignored the vote of no confidence and turned toward the Choktri, speaking slowly for the benefit of the translator.

"Perhaps we should consider an interim solution in view of the complexity of the questions before us."

The translator produced a series of scraping noises that always set his teeth on edge, but Nathan noticed a slight stirring among the twelve Choktri. Was he on the right track or was he on the verge of offending them?

"We propose a temporary agreement to allow construction and testing of the installation, during which period you and your successors can evaluate what might constitute adequate payment for a permanent arrangement."

There was no question this time that he had stirred up the Choktri, to say nothing of the human team. Diane Fallon was staring at him with a stunned expression, Kwami Jordan had leaned forward and covered his face with his hands, and Peri Ravanthani had grabbed his arm, his face contorted by rage. "You imbecile! No one is going to invest in a multi-billion credit installation without a long term understanding."

Nathan ignored him. If he was wrong, it was too late now. If he was right, he had to press the point before he was stopped. "I suggest a test period equivalent to that which you granted the Droogee for the facility in which our delegation is currently housed."

There was a low rumble as the Choktri rather hastily, for Choktri, conferred. Terpat addressed the translator at last. Ravanthani had settled back, but his expression said that Nathan was a dead man, at least in terms of his career.

"The human request is reasonable and acceptable to this committee. The Droogee transferred universal credits to us in full payment of their lease." He named a surprisingly modest sum. "We propose a similar rate in your case, proportionate to the actual dimensions which you decide to occupy."

Nathan did some quick mental arithmetic. It was a bargain, if he was right.

"And what would be the duration of the lease?"

Terpat never hesitated. "Five hundred local years. With an option to renew for the same period if a permanent arrangement has still not been agreed upon by both parties."

Nathan settled back in his seat, so relieved that he was suddenly aware of his own heartbeat. To his right, Ravanthani's expression was changing. He was a small minded man, but not unintelligent. "We find those terms most acceptable." His voice shook with excitement, like that of a man who has just been reprieved from a death sentence.

Success had come so suddenly that it took a while for their emotions to catch up to the human negotiators. Ravanthani became positively convivial although Nathan knew he was already trying to decide how to phrase his reports to accrue the most credit to himself without actually telling lies. He didn't care. Ravanthani would give Nathan a glowing evaluation to keep him quiet and they'd both move a rung upward. That was the way things went.

Connie Layton found him standing at the entrance to the compound, staring across the barren landscape at the massive form of the warren. "So you found the magic bullet after all."

He smiled and put an arm around her. "Actually, it was all because of you."

"Modesty isn't your strong suit, Nathan."

"Nothing modest about it. The mistake we were making was looking for a solution exclusively within the Choktri frame of reference. You were the one who kept telling me that they function very much like we do, that only the details were different."

"I don't follow."

"The Choktri wanted to reach an agreement. They knew that we were going to give them extremely favorable terms. They also knew that there was a way around their inability to sign a permanent agreement. Permanent means something slightly different, in their case. Permanent means forever. They couldn't possibly commit themselves to anything that would be binding on their race until the end of eternity."

Connie nodded. "I get it. But why didn't they just tell us that?"

Nathan smiled. "I think I know the answer to that too, but I can't prove it."

He let the silence stretch until she nudged him with an elbow. "So tell me, man with all the answers."

Nathan chuckled. "I think they just wanted to know if we were smart enough to figure it out on our own."

Games Peoples Play

I'd been on Averis for the equivalent of a Terran month, and I'd been thoroughly briefed before leaving Earth, but I still felt queasy whenever I saw street merchants toasting their own entrails over a slow fire and hawking bite sized pieces to passersby. I know that the Averi grow replacements before their body expels the old set and that it's analogous to human women cutting off their long hair and selling it to wigmakers, but somehow this seems much more personal. I'm told that the resulting snack is relatively tasteless and has virtually no food value, but it's considered good luck to consume the entrails of others, although bad luck indeed to eat one's own.

Averis is a pre-spaceflight world. In fact, their technological expertise is roughly equivalent to that of Earth in the early 18th Century, which would make their culture a potentially superb market for our reinvigorated industrial base. Trade negotiations weren't my specialty, and technically I was still assigned to the diplomatic corps back on Earth, but I had pulled a few strings to get myself temporarily reassigned here for "educational" purposes. I had dealt with more than a dozen visiting races during the past four years, but encounters on Earth were invariably in a climate controlled embassy and the artificial surroundings made it difficult to really comprehend a truly non-human psychology.

I wanted to see at least one alien race in situ, and while a posting to the Pulagi homeworld would have been my first choice, the plum assignments had all gone to senior diplomats and political appointees. Averis was much less attractive, a comparatively primitive culture whose inhabitants were humanoid, but only if you stretched the term to the limits of elasticity. In their relaxed posture, they were about the same height as a human adult, but much wider and deeper, hunched forward suggesting a Neanderthal with elephantiasis.

My morning ritual was a brisk walk after breakfast and before reporting to my office, choosing a different part of the city on each occasion. There was a pushcart on almost every corner, selling woven wares, wood carvings, kitchen utensils, and a wide variety of fresh vegetables and fruits, cooked or raw. Humans can't eat Averi food; it won't kill you but it won't provide nourishment either, and you'd probably end up in the infirmary. Even if our biochemistry had been compatible, I think I'd have drawn the line at entrails, lucky or otherwise. An adult Averi only sheds his or her intestines two or three times per local year, a protracted process during which they were confined to their beds for as long as twenty local days. The scarcity kept the prices at a high enough level that even highly placed professionals would take time off their normal jobs to rent a street cart for an hour and peddle their superfluous body parts in one of the many small open marketplaces.

I had just finished walking through the waterfront area and was on my way to my office when Ambassador Krassner hailed me from a side corridor. "Shaver! Where have you been? I've been looking all over for you."

My daily habit was well known to the ambassador, whose powers of exaggeration turned snacks into banquets and misunderstandings into catastrophes. His aversion to physical exertion made it unlikely that he'd looked very hard. "I went down to watch the night trawlers unloading."

The Averi were herbivorous, like every other animate life form on the planet. The oceans were inhabited by creatures that looked surprisingly similar to Terran fish, although they rarely grew as long as half a meter, but they were left undisturbed by the local fisherfolk. There was virtually no such thing as a predator/prey relationship in the sea, or the land either. There were no carnivores anywhere on Averis, or at least none that we'd heard of. The planet enjoyed monotonously benign weather with almost no detectible seasonal variation, and the vegetation was lush and productive throughout the year. All of the animal forms, including the Averi themselves, had reproduction rates just high enough to maintain the population, and on the rare occasions when they outgrew the food supply, they simply died off until balance was restored. But that was extremely rare. The locals harvested plankton from the oceans and had a highly developed agricultural industry, but left so much produce unharvested that they could have doubled their population without experiencing shortages. They simply chose not to through some form of consensus we had yet to understand.

"Ligamus and his entourage want to meet with us tomorrow. We need to work out a negotiating strategy."

I raised my eyebrows. "What's wrong with what we've already proposed? Ligamus seemed to find it reasonable enough. They've already provided us with a list of the goods they'd like to purchase, and we've suggested the general range of products we'd like them to export. We won't have to strategize much of anything until they're ready to talk about exchange rates and delivery schedules."

"I think we need to be more proactive. We've been in talks for more than a local year already."

"Well, the Averi move at a slower pace than we do, and they aren't particularly materialistic. The Pulagi discovered them about six generations back, and they still don't show any interest in advancing into a technological age. Not one of them has even been off their planet yet." In fact, they seemed profoundly disinterested in space travel. They weren't face with population pressure or a strong competitive drive, so there was no motivation for them to look to the stars . Averis would have made a great vacation spot for humans, if there had been anything to see or do.

"You don't need to remind me how backward they are. I've been here longer than you have."

Not much longer, I hoped, and he certainly hadn't been here long enough to understand the Averi. Krassner sounded offended and I was reminded that he wasn't happy about my presence either. I'd had considerably more experience dealing with alien cultures than he, admittedly only through their visits to Earth, and some of his staff had started to defer to my judgment rather than his. I sighed, but silently, and tried to mend fences.

"You're right, obviously. I just meant that they have a more casual attitude toward the process." I didn't point out that most of the goods they were interested in were for leisure time activities, rather than things that would radically change their living or working habits.

"Well, let's not lose focus. We're here for a purpose and I don't intend to let our side down."

I ignored the implication that I was shirking my responsibilities. Krassner was hardly a fortuitous choice for ambassador or trade negotiator, an indifferent administrator with only a minimal understanding of the economic issues involved, virtually no comprehension of Averi psychology, and a well developed case of species chauvinism. He thought of the Averi as mildly retarded humans and even made a point of talking ponderously slowly when he was addressing them . For that matter, he treated his own staff as though they were interns under his guidance rather than experts whose job was to guide him.

"We're all here for the same purpose, Paul. What is it that you think we should be doing to move things along?"

His face twisted slightly as he tried to figure out whether or not I was criticizing him, then magnanimously decided in my favor. "I'm convening the full staff for a strategy session later this morning. I want proposals from every department head on ways to expedite and expand the trade pact. I realize that you are here more or less as an observer, but since your salary is charged against my budget, I think it only fair that you participate. You've dealt with aliens like these in the past, after all."

I bristled at the suggestion that all aliens were alike, but Krassner had already turned away, his message delivered, my compliance assumed. I found myself suspended between amused exasperation and frustrated anger, decided to go with the former, and walked straight to my office. Sometimes I found human psychology every bit as perplexing as that of non-humans.

"The difficulty is that the Averi don't sense the passage of time the same way we do." Janice Rudzinski, head of xenopsychology, was answering Krassner's question, but she was looking at me. "Almost the entire planet is locked into an endlessly prolonged summer. The Averi have a very long lifespan by human standards and they usually don't reproduce until quite late in their lives, so they lack the cues that human adults experience by watching their kids grow up. Their society is stagnant, and they're perfectly content to keep it that way."

Nguyen Tho, the socio-patternist, shook his head. "They're stable, not stagnant. There's no sign of decay that we've been able to detect, and there are signs of progress, though they're glacierlike by our standards. The population has in fact increased over the past ten generations, although only by a fraction of a percent. When the Pulagi first contacted them, they accepted the existence of space traveling races readily and created the institutions to deal with the situation, and they did so calmly and efficiently. Remember, even though they are loosely organized into separate political entities, it's mostly a geographical convenience. They have no true concept of nationalism and the idea of exchanging ambassadors was completely new to them. Even their internal trade remains basically a barter system. The value of an item fluctuates from individual to individual, even from day to day, far more so than the variations to which we're accustomed. They don't use currency of any sort, and there's no abstract system to assign relative values."

"But they've traded with other cultures before," protested Podhyana, one of the commercial delegates.

Tho nodded. "As I said, they're adaptable. But all of their trade to date has been unstructured. The Ursli arrived with a varied cargo that happened to include a few items the Averi liked. They traded them for wood carvings and some of those elaborate silken webs they build in the corners of their houses."

"Neither of which are of much interest to us," interrupted Krassner.

Tho nodded again, dismissively. "The point is, when the Ursli came back the second time, they couldn't make a deal, not even with the same items that they were able to move the time before. Once the novelty was gone, the merchandise lost its value."

"So we have to provide more practical items." Krassner stood up from the conference table and began pacing back and forth. Apparently he thought this made him look dynamic, but in practice it was forced, nervous, and distracting. "We sell them things they can't make themselves, automated harvesting machines, gyrocars, computers."

I sighed, audibly this time, but only those near me could hear. Rudzinski was the first to object. "We've covered this ground before. They won't use computers. Computers think inorganically and they find that idea obscene."

"Computers don't think!" protested someone from the technical staff, but we all ignored him.

"They're not interested in gyrocars either," said Tho. "We suggested them during one of our first sessions because it was obvious that their mechanized transportation system was, well, almost non-existent. They told us that they were never in any particular hurry to go from one place to another, and they were mildly horrified at the prospect of cutting roads through their forests. They did express some interest when we suggested improvements to the design of their plankton trawlers, but they've already started to make those modifications themselves."

"Well, then, how about communications equipment? They're spread out all over the planet and they still communicate by telegraph."

"Same objection as transportation," replied Tho. "They're never in so much of a hurry to talk to one another that they have any interest in personal phones."

"Are you seriously trying to say that we have nothing to offer these people except games?" Krassner looked from one face to another, searching for an answer he wasn't going to find.

The Averi civilization had developed almost completely without competition. It wasn't totally absent, of course; they strutted and posed to attract the most desirable mates, and matched themselves against one another in other ways. But their educational system, though quite advanced, did not use grading of any sort, not even pass/fail. They had no sports, organized or otherwise, the gap between their wealthiest and poorest citizens was negligible because they valued all useful work equally, and since they didn't have nations or contrasting political systems, they had never had a war and didn't maintain any military force. Violence was comparatively rare, though not unheard of, but the most common motive was what we would call crimes of passion rather than for material gain.

Shortly after the permanent human mission arrived on Averis, two low level functionaries had gotten into the habit of eating their lunch on the gently sloping beach a few blocks from the embassy. One day they were bored and started playing tic-tac-toe in the sand, a couple Averi wandered over to watch, and the rest, as they say, is history.

The concept of gaming must have appealed to some deeply suppressed competitive urge because within days you could see the locals playing the game all over the city, and within weeks it had spread across the planet. The senior consul at the time, Krassner's predecessor, had been quick to realize the implications, and the next ship from Earth carried scores of sets of checkers, chess, Go, backgammon, decks of cards, dice, and a variety of popular board games. The Averi now had bingo parlors and pool halls and gaming clubs where poker and Star Monopoly were played at adjacent tables.

It was like distributing drugs to addicts. Games were the only human artifacts for which the Averi had more than a casual interest, and Consul Koenitz had already completed most of the groundwork for a formal trade agreement before a serious illness had forced her to return to Earth.

Unfortunately, Krassner was openly unhappy with the prospect of a Terran-Averi commercial relationship whose cornerstone consisted of amusements, and he was determined to transform it in order to prove he was the right man for the job.

"We need to uphold the dignity of the human race. I want to establish a healthy trade mission, not a toy shop!"

So even though we already had what we believed was a good basis for an ongoing trading partnership, Krassner browbeat us into discussing possible alternatives. Every suggestion he made was impractical or inappropriate, but as soon as the staff convinced him that one proposal was unworkable, he'd throw up another. "I don't understand you people! You've become as passive as the natives!"

We adjourned for lunch, all of us exhausted intellectually if not physically, and I'm not sure how the afternoon session would have fared if we'd been forced to go through with it. Some of my co-workers were on the verge of conceding points just to get some peace and quiet, and others were ready to fire back angrily and possibly endanger their careers. Fortunately, we were spared either alternative because Krassner managed to pick up a local virus, probably from contaminated food.

Disease was not unknown on Averis, although it was rare enough that the Averi had never felt the need to build hospitals or train medical specialists. The most common was a viral infection that caused the secretion of a particularly unpleasant looking fluid from all over their bodies, the local equivalent of the common cold. Averi germs and viruses could not directly attack humans; but they did occasionally cause some indirect problems. When the human body detected an infection, it made its usual effort to deal with intruders. That resulted in an elevated temperature, sometimes dangerously high, even though the virus itself died within hours of finding itself in an inhospitable host.

Krassner broke out into a sweat as we were leaving the cafeteria and collapsed before he reached the conference room. More than one face expressed relief, and a few were positively delighted. I have to admit to feeling a degree of satisfaction myself.

The medics took him to the dispensary. The most important thing was to lower his body temperature. Once that was stabilized, he'd be safe enough, although it would be at least two or three days before he could get out of bed. I felt a mildly guilty pleasure at the thought which, alas, was short lived.

Kanikrades, the Protocol Officer, tracked me down in the Library. "Nathan, we need to talk."

There was an intense look on his face that should have warned me I wasn't going to like whatever it was that he was about to say.

"What's the problem, Stefano?"

"There's a meeting scheduled with Ligamus tomorrow morning."

I nodded. "I knew that. Nkambi is perfectly capable of filling in for Krassner." In fact, Susan was a much better choice and should have been Ambassador rather than Vice-Consul.

"She would be, if she could get back Krassner sent her over to the other side of the continent to see if there was enough cultural variation to justify a subsidiary mission."

I had known that she was gone, but it had slipped my mind. "Can't you call her back?"

"Sure, but there's no way she can reach us in time. And if we have to postpone the meeting, Ligamus will put us off for weeks. Krassner would be furious, even though it's not our damned fault that he's incapacitated, and frankly the chance of having a meeting without him around to complicate matters is too good to miss."

I found myself nodding. "Good point. So who's going to fill in as chief negotiator?"

Kanikrades looked uncomfortable. "We just caucused and decided that it should be you." I suppose it shouldn't have caught me by surprise, but it did. I stared at him blankly, and he rushed on before I could think of anything to say. "You have more experience than anyone on the staff, and technically you don't report to the ambassador's office. That leaves you more freedom to maneuver than the rest of us."

He was right. As an observer, I was outside the chain of command. Krassner could complain about me, and he probably would, but he didn't have access to my personnel dossier and he couldn't file an adverse evaluation. On the other hand, he could make the balance of my stay on Averis considerably less pleasant if he chose to do so.

"I don't know, Stefano. I'm not authorized to make policy or determine trade terms."

He shook his head. "Wrong. In the absence or incapacity of the two ranking heads of mission, the senior staff is empowered to make a temporary appointment with all the authority of the ambassador himself. It was assumed that we would choose one of our own number, but there's nothing in the regulations that requires that."

" Every one of you has been on Averis longer than I have. Do you really think this is a good idea?"

He nodded his head, but his eyes betrayed his uncertainty.

I have to confess that I felt pretty smug after I'd recovered from the original shock. Although I'd been involved in trade negotiations in the past, it had always been in a supporting role. This time I was going to be able to make decisions rather than suggest them. It was a bit of a letdown to realize that in the long run, what I did would make little difference. Ligamus and the rest of the Averi were interested in the results but not the process. They would be genuinely excited once the goods arrived, but the meetings and the mechanics that led to that goal held no attraction for them. They were equally enthusiastic about selling their used intestines, but that didn't mean that they enjoyed the process of disconnecting and expelling them.

I thought about that image and shuddered a bit, but then I thought about it some more. And something clicked.

I spent a restless night, but when I rose the following morning, I felt certain that I was on to something. While taking my morning walk, I thought about conferring with some of the staff, but frankly I was worried that they'd revoke my appointment if they knew what I was planning to do. That made me wonder if perhaps I was indeed taking too big a chance, so I told myself that I would keep my options open, that my original plan had been demoted to an option, that I would wait until Ligamus made his presentation and then decide how to proceed.

It was the Averi turn to play host so we met in a very large meeting hall in the city, actually a communal eating place where the Averi could come and graze in small groups. Ligamus was accompanied by an even dozen advisers, while I had brought along only Kanikrades, Tho, Rudzinski, and two trade specialists whose names I was constantly forgetting, or mixing up.

As host, Ligamus was obligated to speak first and he did, at great length, but with little substance. He expressed admiration for the achievements of the human race, appreciation for our interest in trading with his people, and amazement at the speed with which we'd learned their language. Our trade goods would be welcomed, he assured us, and he was confident that it would be only a matter of time until we were able to devise an exchange system. He expressed his sympathy for Ambassador Krassner's misfortune and his confidence that I would prove more than able to serve in his place.

He talked for more than two hours, and even making allowances for cultural differences, I thought he was probably just as much a stuffed shirt as was Krassner. I knew what motivated the Ambassador, but I was just guessing about the Averi. I could play it safe and follow the script Krassner had provisionally approved and eventually the meeting would end with little progress but without disaster. I'd had an inspiration, though. I was pretty sure Krassner wasn't going to like my idea, but on the other hand, Ligamus might find it irresistible.

I stood up when it was my turn to speak, and the words spilled out of me so quickly that I guess I never really intended to stray from my original plan. I heard sharp intakes of breaths from my companions and a couple of startled murmurs, but no one interrupted. When I sat down, there was silence. The humans were stunned; the Averi were, I believe, intrigued.

Ligamus requested a short adjournment so that he could confer with his colleagues. That had never happened before. All of the previous meetings with the Averi had proceeded, at least on their part, as though they'd been rehearsed to the smallest detail, which might well be the case. None of my companions spoke to me except for Janice, who asked if I knew what I was doing.

"Probably not," I admitted. "But it seemed like a good idea at the time."

A few minutes later, we reconvened, and Ligamus surprised us all.

"You did what!"

Krassner was so livid that I thought he might have a relapse. His agitation was so intense and immediate that he'd come to my quarters rather than summon me to his office.

"Please sit down, Paul. You don't look at all well. I've written a report explaining my strategy. There was an element of risk involved, of course, but there always is in this kind of situation."

"You don't have the authority to commit us to such a ridiculous program!" Not only was he not sitting, he was storming back and forth across my sitting room.

"Not now, I don't. But I did at the time. And it worked. Ligamus has provisionally agreed to the terms of exchange that I outlined, and the Averi are willing to accept the first shipment as soon as we can get it here."

"But we could end up losing the value of the entire shipment!" He was waving his fists through the air now. "You're gambling with the entire future of trade with this planet!"

"Calm yourself, Ambassador. If you look at the terms of the agreement carefully, you will see that the Averi agree to trade directly for the first quarter of any cargo at a rate which is actually quite favorable to us."

"But they could end up getting the other three quarters for nothing at all!"

"That would be the worse case scenario, yes. Our expenses would be covered in that case, just barely, but we'd make virtually no profit."

"If there's no profit, there's no incentive for companies back on Earth to ship their wares here." I'm not sure whether he was growing calmer or just running out of energy. His pacing slowed, then stopped, and he sat down heavily in my one good chair.

"On the other hand, in the best case scenario, they'll make a profit beyond anything in their experience." I paused to let that sink in. "In practice, the results will fall somewhere between the two extremes. Every ship that comes here will benefit, Paul, but the take will vary from trip to trip."

He sat forward in his seat, his head down. "How will I ever explain this to the Secretary?"

"Blame me if you want to. Hanson will believe you; he and I have tangled in the past. Or if you think I'm right, tell him I was acting under your instructions and take the credit for yourself."

His voice changed, became resigned and possibly a bit crafty. "Tell me again how this is supposed to work."

"It's simple. We've agreed on a table of equivalences between our goods and the items we want in exchange. Some of the matches are admittedly disproportionately in their favor, but on the other hand, we have at least a temporary edge during the actual trading process."

"You really expect to play dice using cargo as the stake?"

"Dice, or poker, or chess. The more complex the game, the bigger the wager. The Averi aren't interested in the process of trade but, thanks to us, they like playing games. Games are the only stimulus we've discovered that actually stirs them out of their lethargy."

"But we won't be able to guarantee more than a break even."

"No, we won't." I smiled, actively enjoying myself. "The big conglomerates back on Earth all stress the work ethic and the need to put aside childish things and act maturely. Well, this time everything is going to depend on how good they are at playing games." An image popped into my head and I chuckled. "Better yet, maybe they should send their kids along to do the negotiating for them."